Tony Bury, born 1972 in Northampton, England, has had a passion for writing songs, poems and short stories since an early age. He has taken it more seriously since having kids, writing several children's books and screen plays. *The Intervention* is his third novel in the Alex Keaton series, following on from *Intervention Needed.*

The Intervention

The Intervention is the third Alex Keaton novel.

Also by Tony Bury

Intervention Forgiven
Intervention Needed

Tony Bury

The Intervention

Vanguard Press

VANGUARD PAPERBACK

© Copyright 2016
Tony Bury

The right of Tony Bury to be identified as author of
this work has been asserted by him in accordance with the
Copyright, Designs and Patents Act 1988.

All Rights Reserved

No reproduction, copy or transmission of this publication
may be made without written permission.
No paragraph of this publication may be reproduced,
copied or transmitted save with the written permission of the
publisher, or in accordance with the provisions
of the Copyright Act 1956 (as amended).

Any person who commits any unauthorised act in relation to
this publication may be liable to criminal
prosecution and civil claims for damages.

A CIP catalogue record for this title is
available from the British Library.

ISBN 978 178 465 175 6

*Vanguard Press is an imprint of
Pegasus Elliot MacKenzie Publishers Ltd.*
www.pegasuspublishers.com

First Published in 2016

**Vanguard Press
Sheraton House Castle Park
Cambridge England**

Printed & Bound in Great Britain by CMP (uk) Limited

To all my friends and family.
Never give up on your dreams – anything is possible.

Alex Keaton is back.

It's time to finish what Jack started.

Chapter One

"Who gives this child so that he may serve to the hand of our god, so that he may fight the fight of the righteous and the true?"

"We do." The group of women that had gathered in the sacrificial room spoke in unison.

"We sacrifice this child in order that he will be reborn a warrior of heaven. His selfless act, and the act of our congregation will help god almighty drive Satan from our world, and the after world."

"Praise be to god." The congregation spoke again.

"Praise be to god." Preacher Alastair Lee held a new-born baby to the air as if showing him for the first time.

"Praise be to god, it is through his direction and his giving's that we rejoice in the rebirth of this child. He who gave his own child to sacrifice so that we may follow in his footsteps. We give this child unto thee."

The preacher placed the baby back onto the table. He picked up the knife from the table next to him. The knife was made of steel with a gold handle, at the crest of the handle was a lion's head.

"The Canterbury knife, this knife is forged from the steel that pierced the body of Our Saviour. And is adorned with the head of a lion so that strength will be passed through us and into this child. With this knife comes rebirth and from rebirth he will be born into the arms of our lord."

"Re birth, re birth, and re birth" The crowd had now started to chant the words back to the preacher.

"Go with god, stand by the side of the Almighty against the sinners of this world and the next. Go with God my son. Become the warrior you were born to be."

The preacher held the knife high in the air and with one swift movement brought it down and pierced the heart of the new born baby.

"Praise him, praise him" The congregation continued to chant back at the preacher, there was a round of applause that had started as they all watched the life go out of the child. The tears in the eyes of the congregation were not ones of sorrow but of joy and rejoice.

"Our son, born unto me and Sister Michelle, is now and will forever be a warrior of heaven. We have given this sacrifice so that his life in heaven, will be at the hand of our father and we will one day be re united in heaven."

"Praise him, praise him"

The baby was wrapped in a black gown and taken out of the room by one of the women that had been standing next to the preacher. She also, as with the whole congregation had been wearing a similar black gown to the one now adorning the baby.

At their induction to the religion Preacher Alastair had presented them each with the gown of glory. A black hooded gown, made of black velvet.

It had been made clear to them that when they were wearing this gown they could be seen by heaven. When wearing the gown, god would know to turn his attention to them. Their god would be able to see their sacrifice's that they made on earth, in order to secure their place in heaven.

"Praise him indeed. We have sent our son to heaven. It is now time for reflection. Time to think of those we have sent to stand side by side with our lord. As he continues in his battle to save all our soul's. It is time to pray." The whole room fell silent as they bowed their heads in prayer. Sister Casandra who had taken the baby out of the room and placed him in the ceremonial coffin returned and stood next to the preacher. She watched as all the heads were bowed in prayer apart from hers and Preacher Alastair. She reached out and held his hand. He pulled her a little closer and continued to rub her palm gently. There was a moment of chemistry between them and then he let go.

"After reflection comes rejoice, rejoice in our sacrifice and rejoice in the knowing, that god is watching us. He who looks over us, has seen what we have done and will indeed be rejoicing in Heaven, with our son. For today we have taken another step in our Journey ne Quest to internal glory."

The congregation looked up from their prayer. There were smiles and congratulations all around and the crowd started to disperse.

"Now ladies please do not forget there is a reading after supper tonight, that Sister Gretna is going to read to us, I am so looking forward to this, so please ensure we are all on time." There was some acknowledgement as the ladies all left the room apart from Sister Casandra and Preacher Alastair.

"Sister Michelle has been so lucky to be able to help you give a child to our Lord Preacher Alastair"

"Sister Casandra, it's just Alastair. I do not want to be labelled as anything other than who I am, and who I am is just a messenger." There was a pause before Sister Casandra plucked up enough courage to ask the next question.

"I know I have been asking for a while, but when will it be my turn, Alastair, when will I be blessed with the chance to give life to a warrior or a saviour."

Preacher Alastair pulled the robe down from around her head to uncover a young barely sixteen-year-old blonde girl. She was stunningly beautiful with deep green eyes.

"I was saving this for after the reading tonight Sister Casandra, but tonight you will be called upon to the bed of our lord. Where with love, and hope, we may join together in the creation of a child. A child which will either serve with us on this mortal world as all her sisters will have done before her. Or a child which may join the fight against evil. Tonight you are to come to me so that I may do my duty to god."

"Oh Alastair, I am so happy, I have been praying for so long for this." Sister Casandra leaped forward and hugged the preacher.

"Your wait is over my child."

Alastair led Casandra out of the room and into the main hall way of the main house.

The house was big, eleven bedrooms and at least three sitting rooms, the garage had been turned into the sacrificial room and there had been an extension on the kitchen in order that the whole family could sit at the table to eat at the same time. There were a few out buildings in the grounds where the older sisters would stay. The house was reserved for the younger sisters and their children. To date there were twenty-seven women with eight daughters under the age of fifteen living in the house. With one male. Alastair Lee. Alastair had formed his religion over the past twelve years and now was an aging forty three-year-old male. Around six foot two, red headed and his fitness had seen better days. He and Sister Casandra headed towards the kitchen where there were numerous people preparing foods. They smiled at everyone as they entered the room and then began to join in the preparation. The baby had been taken away by a couple of the eldest sisters and buried in their plot in the garden. There was no further ceremony involved once the soul had been taken to heaven.

Supper was a well-orchestrated event and they had all been completing this task for a number of years. There hadn't been anyone new joining the religion for over four years now, so they were a very closed circle. The women were from all walks of life and ethnicity. Nobody was turned away from the religion as long as they believed in everything that the Preacher had told them.

Within twenty minute's supper was prepared and they all sat down to eat. Preacher Alastair had blessed the food and the day, he blessed that they had once again supported the lord in his fight against evil and sent a warrior to heaven.

There was a lot of talk at the table about religion and their own sacrifices to making the world a better place. Preacher Alastair each morning gave them an update on the outside world and the fight that was still going on. There was total faith in his word. He explained how the world had become a dangerous place and that god needed their sacrifice and support now more than ever. None of the women or children ever left the complex. It was only a few acres wide, but whilst they were there, they were under his protection and no harm would come of them.

When supper was over and the whole family had cleared the table they all adjourned to one of the living rooms. There were various sofas and bean bags placed all around the room so it would comfortably accommodate the audience. It had the feeling of a relaxed coffee shop or book club where they would be listening to an author speak on his latest novel.

"Once we have settled, Sister Gretna can begin."

They all took their seats quietly and looked onward at the Sister, Alastair was sitting just behind her and to the right so that the whole room could see him.

"My Sisters, and our saviour. It is so wonderful to be given the opportunity to speak and read from our workings. Especially on a sacrificial day which is so holy and special to us. It is with regret though that before we start, I need to let you know that Sister Eleanor has left us. She has returned to the outside world, no longer able to keep the strength and courage to continue on this path. She has been drawn back into the world. The world surrounded by Satan and all his followers. May gods light keep her safe and show her the way back home to us."

"Praise be to god," the women and children we in unison once more.

"Praise be to god indeed, I wanted to start this evenings reading with one of our own, one from Preacher Alastair" They all turned to look at the preacher smiling for his approval.

"So be it," Alastair Lee waved his hands in front of him.

There was an impromptu round of applause at his agreement to the reading. Sister Gretna began her reading.

"God teaches us to be loyal, through his words and the actions of his son. He teaches us above everything else to be loyal to each other. There was a time, before I was called upon where my loyalty was lost to me. I knew neither of the loyalty of love, or loyalty of relationships. It was at this time god almighty chose to appear to me and gave me direction. He said unto me that I must lead the vessels of life into service. I must sacrifice my place at his right hand, so that I can show them the way." The preacher looking at the audience wiped his eyes as if to show that tears were forming.

"Alastair please read this to us. It comes so much better from you." There was an agreement from the room and they all looked directly at him. He took the book and found his place.

"It was then I knew my true calling. I knew I was needed, and what I would have to do in order to help save the kingdom of heaven. My hope would have been to serve at his hand in the fight, but god had a higher purpose for me. God whispered the words to me that today the world lives by.

Be unto one master on earth for he will show you the light and the direction to heaven.

Give unto me the sons of the vessels for they will serve at my right hand in the battles that are and are to come.

The bloodline of god is within in you. Pass this bloodline to the sons and daughters as they start their journey with me. For only children of god or vessels from where they came may enter through the gates of heaven.
Make the sons strong of birth with the heart of a lion so that they may fight at my side.

The daughters are to be virtuous so that they may stay strong for the birth of warriors.

My loyalty was no longer in question, when I heard these words, I knew they were truth. A truth that can only be spoken by god.

I wandered for months on the quest for the vessels for a sign to see who, who were sinners and who were prepared to take his word and his wisdom. It was then I was blessed, blessed to have found Sister Teresa."

Everyone turned to Sister Teresa, she had been sitting at the back of the room. There was a smile in every direction towards her.

"Sister Teresa led me here. Here to her home where I could open her heart to god. She too had been through dark times over the previous years. Her faith had been questioned, but never her loyalty, no her loyalty was strong. Those around her had been deceitful in their actions and she was ready to bring around change to the world with the support of our lord." The book was closed now as he continued to speak.

"It reminds me of a story I was once told about a child. When a child is born into the world for the first few minutes, before it drops back off to sleep. It looks at its guardians and can mimic everything they do, from closing eyes, mouthing words and even moving hands. It is taught by the people that have unconditional love for them. Like god does for you, for all of you. He sees loyalty in every one of you. If you are open and true to him he will guide you and in turn you mimic him. He shows you that you will always be loved. He will show you how to act and how to behave. But once you have tasted the darkness, once the world has been questioned it is so much harder to get back to those teaching's. A new born baby forgets all they have seen when it awakes in the real world for the first time. The baby has started to taste the darkness after that first sleep. As whilst it is asleep its sub conscious can hear, smell, feel. This is because the world is too big for them, and no child or parent can know everything which is true. To protect them from the world and the darkness we learn, in order to stay committed, we must stay together. We must find our place in the world however small and keep together those that matter. The world is a big place which when they are faced with it. It brings doubt into their hearts no matter how small they are." Preacher Alastair knew he had the room. He always had the room, they fed off his every word.

"Doubt is a harsh word. We can never be in doubt with our mission and our purpose in this world. We are here to serve the lord in whichever way we can." There was an agreement of nodding heads.

"Some more Alastair, read some more."

"Now I don't want to pull the spot light from Gretna."

"No Alastair, more would be lovely. We very rarely get this opportunity for you to read to us."

"Okay, one more passage. Let it be about something that is close to us all, love." Preacher Alastair opened the book.

"Love, love not only as the love with have for each other, or even the love we have for the lord. But love in its entirety. For if it was not for the sinner then we would never know the deep affection we have for the saint. Love is everything to us and we must remember that out of love, comes togetherness, closeness and meaning of life. But love can be blinding. On our path we need to be able to identify true love from false love. For the sinner has many faces." The preacher closed the book.

"That statement about identifying love was a question of faith for me. I prayed hard on this until the lord spoke to me. He showed me how to identify true love, love that had an unconditional nature. For me it was in the eyes. If you look hard and long enough you can see directly into someone's soul. Something I have shared with all of you. Whilst we are here together we know we are loved, we know we are safe under the protection of his lord."

At the back of the room one of the younger sisters raised her hand.

"Sister Catherine do you have something to say? You know our policy we want you to speak up child."

"Father Alastair, we know we are under the protection of the lord. And when we are at prayer he can see us because we wear the gown of glory. But how do we know he is protecting us now? We are not wearing it?"

There were smiles from the room. This question had been asked a lot over the past twelve years and usually by the younger members of the congregation.

"Because my daughter, our complex is cloaked by the gown of glory. It is true our lord knows to look in our direction when we wear the gown. It is us standing out to him even more, but he is always watching over us." Preacher Alastair was smiling at the child.

"Imagine it is Sunday, and we always have ice-cream on Sundays don't we?"

"Yes Father."

"So when Sister Teresa brings out the vats of ice-cream there is oh so many flavours, vanilla, strawberry, choc fudge ripple … loads of them. You watch as they are all placed on the table don't you, I know you Catherine, it's your favourite dessert."

The was a giggling from all the younger children

"And if I am not mistaken, when rocky road comes out you almost pounce at it…" The giggling continued.

"The rocky road is cloaked with the gown of glorious yumminess I believe… you can see all the other ice-creams you know they are yummy too but when that one stands out … you look a little deeper."

The laughter was more around the room now and Sister Catherine sat back on her beanbag.

"I think that is enough for one evening well at least from me."

There was a unison of no's and one more passage.

"No I think I have stolen enough of Gretna's limelight and it will be good for her to speak to you all. It is time for me to retire."

There was silence across the room. With the words *it is time for me to retire* generally made this happen in anticipation for what followed.

"Our Lord Spoke to me this morning and said today is a good day, it is a good day because not only have we sent our son to stand by his side in the ongoing battle against evil, but today is a day of conception," the older women in the room were all smiling with joy. There was an acceptance that any of them could be called upon tonight.

"And tonight will not only be a night of conception, but one of beginning, where one of the sisters will at last fulfil her journey into womanhood." The crowd turned towards Sister Casandra, they had known her time had been coming and were genuinely glad for her. They saw this as an honour to them all.

"Sister Casandra, the lord has spoken to me, and tonight is your night. The sisters will bathe and prepare you and then you are to come to my chambers." There was a round of applause at this announcement.

The preacher closed the book and left the room.

Three of the older sisters took Casandra out of the room as Sister Gretna continued to read to the others. They led her through the kitchen and up the stairs to one of the bathrooms

"I am so excited."

"There is no talking my child, this is the greatest honour that we can do for our lord. We do not talk before, during or after the event of the conception. The process is simple we are to take you to the bath and bathe you from head to toe. Ensuring that your body has the fragrance of lavender. We then dress you in your Gown of Glory."

"I don't have it, it's down stairs."

"Don't worry one of the sisters will go and retrieve it. You are then to walk to the Preachers chambers. Once inside it is up to the preacher on how to proceed. But you must do as he says. And not speak unless he orders it. He knows the type of warrior or Sister that is needed from this conception. This is all we can tell you."

"But…"

"No more Sister Casandra, this is your time and you have been chosen to give the world an amazing gift."

Sister Casandra smiled to herself all through the bathing. She had been brought there by her mother six years ago and her mother had been chosen twice since then to vessel two warriors for the lord. Her mother had in truth spent a lot of time with the preacher in the attempt to create a child but as he had told them. The lord choses his warriors and Sisters, it was his divine right to decide if this child was going to stay the path or not. For even though they were saints, sinners are and can be born to all.

The whole ceremony had taken about an hour to prepare sister Casandra.

Whilst this was happening the preacher was in his chambers. Nobody came into there unless they had been invited for the act of conception. Or it was Sister Teresa as she was his designated cleaner.

It was more like a suite in a hotel. Big wide screen TV and a bar. Only Sister Teresa knew what was in his room. For when the women were brought in for conception the bar and screen were all covered up. It gave the impression that he lived a solitary life.

They didn't allow alcohol anywhere on the complex. But Sister Teresa had often shared a drink with him of an evening if he was not in the mood to create a warrior.

Preacher Alastair had showered and laid back on the bed, he had popped a blue pill which would help him with the lord's work and watched about twenty minutes of adult movies on the pay per view channel that he had. He knew how long the process had taken and about five minutes before Casandra was due he covered the TV area and bar and then lowered the lights. Playing soft gentle music in the background. The anticipated knock on the door came.

"Come in."

Casandra's gown entered the room. They had all been one size and because she was so petite the gown completely covered her.

"Do you know what is expected of you?"

There was a nod from the hood. The preacher was still over by the music station but turned to walk slowly towards her.

"My Sister, the act of love can take many strange forms. Our lord through me shows me what he wants. If he were to desire for us to create a great warrior from heaven that needed to be prepared for the darkest of wars, he may ask us to do things that would not seem normal. Things that will question our faiths but we are here to do his bidding."

There was another nod from the gown.

"Tonight will be such a night. He is looking for a warrior above all else. And tonight you and I will be creating history. The words you hear will be offensive the acts we do will be hard and violent. But a warrior born in this way will be stronger for our lord. A warrior born in violence will find his place in blood."

The preacher now stood in front of the hooded figure.

"Casandra are you ready to receive," As he said this he lifted his hands to the hood of the cloak.

"Are you?" He started to pull the hood back and in an instance got a flash of long black hair. As the hood fell backwards the preacher could feel the steel of a gun under his chin."

"How many Preacher, how many?"

Chapter Two

"What, what, what are you doing here? Who are you?"

Alex Pushed him backwards onto the bed with the gun firmly still focused on him.

"How many preacher, how many?"

"How many what? What the hell are you doing in my house." The preacher was squirming his way back to the head of the bed.

"How many have you killed? I know you killed your mother, your sister and your wife. Before coming here to start this kind of freak show."

"I didn't kill anyone."

"You killed them, you strangled your mother and raped and murdered your sister." Alex paused. Everyone's first defence. I didn't do it. Something else caught Alex's attention.

"That was the smell wasn't it." Alex paused as she remembered something from the case files.

"That was the reason why the young girl who was just about to give herself to you was smelling of lavender. Not a coincidence that your sister was found raped and murdered in a field of lavender, shortly before your mum died. She was your first wasn't she? How old were you fourteen?"

The preacher was now firmly against the head of the bed and canvasing the room.

"I didn't do anything to my sister."

"Don't talk crap, I have you down for all three of these and we found Eleanor's body, that's at least three women from this institute that we know of. I am guessing that their lives ended in this room. Played a little too hard did we? From the speech earlier you sounded as if that was your perversion. What I don't understand is why you didn't bury the bodies like you have done with the babies?"

The preacher fell silent.

"Yes I know about the babies, I know about the war, and you are single handily trying to save the planet. You see I have been here most of the day, I wish I had known where you were earlier though as I would have been able to save at least one of your victims." Alex had been watching from a distance and there were no windows in the sacrificial room.

"They are not victims they are helping the lord."

"You're as disillusioned as the people who live here and take in your crap."

"What have you done with Sister Casandra?" Alex thought it was rich that he cared for another. Especially given the speech on the way in.

"A favourite is she? I can see that, young, what I would say sixteen? Maybe fifteen? Very similar to your sister."

The preacher was silent again.

"Tell me preacher how did you get these women to fall for you, look at you, you are hardly Richard Gere? Or is it that they were so vulnerable they would believe any crap that was spun to them?"

The preacher didn't answer the question.

"It's your turn now preacher, you need to confess to save your soul. You tell me everything and it will save you."

"Save me?"

Alex stared straight back at him.

"Yes save you." She pulled a file from behind her back and placed it on the bed.

"This is what we know so far, Mother, Sister, Wife, Eleanor, Stacey and we know about the babies, confess the lot and it will save you."

The preacher was still firmly against the head of the bed with Alex standing at the bottom of it. He was still scanning the room. She was between him the door or the window there was no way to get past her.

"Don't think about it, you wouldn't be the first person I have shot." Alex put her hand in her left side pocket and rummaged around she then changed the gun to the other hand and went into the right side pocket and pulled out her badge, for what it was worth nowadays.

"And it's not like I am going to be in trouble for doing it. Tell me it all and it will save you. But it has to be now." The tone of Alex's voice showed that she meant it.

Alastair Lee almost took the view of the badge as the end. If the police where here, then they knew everything and he wasn't going to get away with it any longer. Jail was inevitable as soon as someone broke the inner circle of his cult. He took a moment of reflection and then started to spill his guts.

"My Sister was my first, I loved her I really loved her. She never understood and she didn't love me like that. I told my mother what I had done, and she was going to lock me up. So she was my second, I don't think she ever loved me she just went along with the whole pregnancy, IVF thing because father had said that is what he wanted." There was real hurt in the preacher's voice as he said that. Alex believed that he never felt loved. Probably why he created his own world.

"My sister was born in France and my dad wanted a son to pass the business on to. After my mother was gone I was alone for a while. So I went travelling. Europe, Africa, South America." Alex hadn't picked up on the fact that his sister was born at the institute also. If she had she would have noticed like most girls the C.L. Compassionate and Loving genes were passed on. Very few women got the real dose of what they were experimenting with in the Brown Institute.

"Until I met Layla, she was lovely dark skinned and beautiful. We were married within six months and she came back with me to the US to live. I didn't know that is all she wanted. All she really wanted was a green card to live in the USA. When she told me I couldn't control it. I just killed her."

"You didn't just kill her, you brutally raped her first."

"She deserved it, she was a tramp" This was the real preacher emerging from what had been shown in the grounds of his sanctuary over the last twelve years.

"Then what?"

"Then nothing. I did nothing for a few years. I couldn't work. I couldn't sleep. I would sit up all night watching the god channels on TV. They seemed to be the only things on at two a.m. Normal people spouting crap about what god could do for them, and what he could do for us. The whole congregation were mostly women, they lapped this crap up. I guess it was a feeble mind thing. I watched as the money poured in from these saps and yes I admit I wanted some of it. So I started to go to a few meetings sit in the back ground and watch what they did and how they did it. It was show, don't get me wrong it was a good show. All you needed was a purpose and an angle and something that stood you apart from the crowd. I came up with a religion, one where women only could enter into, then there was never any fear of other men getting involved, as I am sure they would have questioned me more. I watched as the women came and went from these meetings, all looking for something, either someone had died in their family or their husband had left them." The preacher paused at this point.

"Then I met Teresa, poor woman. Her husband of twenty years had left her for his secretary. We got to speaking and she invited me to dinner. Here to this place." It was the first time Alex had seen a smile on his face since entering the room.

"Thought you had won the lottery did you?"

The preacher didn't answer the question.

"I thought it was a good place to form a little circle of believers and between us that is what we did, she had quite a few friends who had been through similar experiences, it would seem men with money, and secretaries are not a good recipe for success. We between us convinced them to move in and sell their houses that helped fund the place and make the changes we needed."

"Huge walls around the estate, cameras at every turn, that sort of thing?"

Again the preacher ignored Alex's question. He fell silent.

"Nothing else to say preacher? I want to know how many people you have killed. I am not particularly interested in the story of your success."

"When you say it will save me? Are you going to let me go?"

It was Alex's turn to not answer a question.

"There are six deaths on the table. Looking through unsolved murders in the region of this house. I am presuming at least another five. And then there are the innocent little children also. I can't imagine how many of them there are. I think if we add a few counts of child rape into the mix also, will probably make you the biggest monster this state has ever seen."

"It's not like I could have."

"Couldn't have what preacher? Stopped yourself? On some level I believe you. I believe you couldn't stop yourself from killing these women. But you, you are the worst kind of murderer. Some murderers attack you in a dark alley or shoot you from a distance and run. They know what they are and so do their victims. You, you have made your victims fall in love with you. Even worship you, you have warped their mind and long after you have stopped they will still believe in what you have done."

"I don't deserve to go to prison for what I have done, I have saved the lives of all the people in this community and made it better for each and every one of them."

Alex knew there was some truth in this. Everything she had seen or heard about cults in the past always led to the point that the people that lived in them were happy. Content. There was just always an underlying scene of madness.

"I am sure what you deserve your god will ensure you get preacher. Time is wearing thin and my partners are outside waiting. A number and then we can move on."

The preacher sat in silence again scanning the room once more to see if he could escape. Alex was a little woman but there was no doubt in his mind that she would pull that trigger if she needed to.

"Seven, it wasn't five more it was seven. There are two Sisters buried on the compound. I stopped burying them because our community got bigger and the bigger it got the more room we needed. Extensions to the house and the out houses and the women that lived here love to garden. I could not risk them finding the bodies whilst they were digging up vegetables or something."

"Why?" Alex found herself asking this question a lot, even though she knew it was in his DNA. Why, was because he was born in the brown institute in Paris. Why, is because Dr Smith and his partners had created him. Although Dr Smith was no longer going to be able to create anymore, she had killed him in the altercation with Alana and Michael Mellor.

"When I formed this place it was not my intention."

"What was your intention?"

"To make some money, maybe for a year or so see what happens. Within such a short time we had a following. They worshipped me and hung on every word that I said. I couldn't help myself. Half of my life I had been ignored by my parents, and my sister and even when I thought I had found someone, it played out that she was just using me for something else. Here I was the something else. I was their leader and their master. And they would all do what I wanted. Teresa had no interest in sex but she made a great partner in this venture. Her husband had seen to it that she was never interested in men. He wasn't a nice man, he was violent and a drunk. His leaving was actually a blessing for her although she couldn't see it at the time. So when we had a few other women in the community. I came up with the story one night at bible reading. Honestly I thought it was a stretch but within a day they were approaching me on how they could help god. How they could send warriors to heaven. Or produce vessels in order to do his duty."

Alex almost started to think that he had done these women a favour.

"I could take my pick."

There was a smug look on his face as he said that. This stopped Alex thinking he had done anyone a favour. This had been all for him. His ego.

"It's nothing to be proud of, what you have done to these women. What happened next?"

"There was a Sister Jackie and things got a little out of hand in the room. She looked so much like my mother did when she was younger. I hadn't really noticed it until we were in here. We were playing games and I had told her that when she was close to climax she was to scream my name so that the lord would know who was assisting her in his work. I hadn't come up with the Gown of Glory at the time. I did after that night. She called out my name but as soon as I heard it and looked at her I could hear my mother's voice and see my mother in front of me. I couldn't help it, I placed my hands around her neck and broke it within seconds."

There was a pause from the preacher

"The rest?"

"The rest? After that had happened I thought that I was going to be found out. We had already closed the outside world to all but me in the community, as I was the only one strong enough to walk amongst the sinners alone. I knew everyone was in bed so I buried Sister Jackie in the garden. The next morning at prayer I told them that she was not strong enough to be a vessel and overnight she had returned to the world of the sinners. We prayed for her and moved on."

"And that was the green light? They just believed what you said?"

The preacher just nodded

"Wow, that was the green light, you can just kill, fuck, manipulate whomever you want whenever you want." The preacher was getting under Alex's skin. Although she also felt the same rage for the women that let him do this.

"I didn't start it for that reason, it just happened."

"It just happened? What about the babies?" The preacher took a pause.

"I didn't start with the view of killing them you know. I said they would be born as warriors of god. At first we had a girl born into the community. She is perfect, and still living here. Then Sister Linda had a son. The baby cried from the time it was born till the time it died. It didn't stop, morning noon and night with the crying. The women used to take turns in looking after it but I could still hear it all the way down here. One night I had had enough I walked down the corridor. Sister Linda was asleep, the baby was still crying in the next room. I took a pillow and stopped the crying. In the morning at service I had told them of the message I had received from god that he was taking the baby to be by his side as they battle was raging on and he needed him. When the next son was born into the community Sister Vera almost handed him over to me. She said she wanted him to do his part. I struggled to do the first one, with the child being so young. Although the Sisters were encouraging me. I found the knife in an old antique store and that's where the story came from. I must admit by now I thought this was going to be the place I was going to spend the rest of my days. I thought that if there were no other males in their lives then there would be no one to fall in love with but me."

"That's sick so you just killed the baby in front of them?"

"We had a service, but to answer your question, yes."

It was Alex's turn to pause and reflect on what she had heard. This was her first hand to hand experience of a cult. These women were almost as mad as the preacher and kind of deserved each other. If they were that gullible then maybe he has done them a favour by getting them off the street.

"Seventeen," Alex wasn't expecting the number.

"What?"

"Seventeen, they have graves outside in the garden."

Seventeen. Ten plus seventeen equals twenty-seven that is what was going through Alex's mind twenty-seven, the bar Deacon. She could have been twenty-eight. Without thinking the trigger in her hand had pulled three times, each time hitting the preacher directly in the chest. Whilst nobody outside the complex would have heard that certainly most of the people in would have. She took the file off the bed and opened it. On the front page was a list starting with his sister and ending with Sister Eleanor. She ticked all of the names and added at the bottom plus two Sisters in the garden and seventeen children also in the garden.

There was already knocking on the door by the time she had done that. The screaming for Alastair had started. Alex placed the file on his chest picked up her badge and walked over and slightly opened the door pointing the gun directly at them.

"Back up ladies." There were half a dozen women on the other side of the door already.

"But Alastair."

"I said back up."

Alex's voice had meant business, the crowd was getting bigger but they were all moving backwards now.

"Where is the nearest communal room?"

"What have you done to preacher Alistair?" Sister Teresa was front and centre by now.

"I said where is the nearest communal room, we go there and I will explain."

"Downstairs," came a voice from the back of the crowd.

"Then let's all go there."

Alex stepped out of the preacher's room and closed the door behind her.

"No one is to go in there until the police arrive is that understood?"

There wasn't an answer from the group but they were going to be following the person with the gun pointed at them all. Alex opened the door to the left of her where a naked Casandra was tied up and gagged.

"Someone please escort this lady also downstairs and get her some clothes."

Everyone did as they were told and headed to the room. There was a lot of silence. Nobody from the outside world was seen in this house. There were mumblings of Alex being the devil or a sinner but none that could be heard above a whisper.

Alex pulled a tape recorder out of her pocket. When she had been seen to be fumbling for her badge in fact she had been pressing the tape recorder on so that she had evidence of his confession.

"Preacher Alastair was not who you all believed him to be." Alex knew not one woman in the room was going to believe her. She couldn't undo his years of work in a matter of minutes.

"He is our saviour, what have you done to him? Is he?"

"Wait, this isn't a question and answers session. As I said he is not who you believed him to be, He killed his sister, his mother, his wife and seven of your fellow sisters that were in this house."

Tears had started already in the crowd. Along with chants of its not true

"I don't believe you," Sister Teresa was front and centre.

"I don't either, you are a sinner." Alex couldn't question that point she had certainly broke a few commandments in the past three months.

"Also he is responsible for the murder of the seventeen children that lay in the garden."

"It's a lie. Preacher Alastair is a voice from god!" Sister Teresa was still backing him to the end. Alex took one look at the woman and knew who she was.

"Sister Teresa I presume, she has deceived you also, she was part of his made up fantasies. I believe she knew everything that had been going on. Including the murder of your sisters."

The room turned to look at Sister Teresa who was nodding her head in disproval.

"It is lies my sisters, she is the Devil, sent here to test you." The crowd had started to question what it was hearing.

"You have a choice lady's? I am going to click play on this recorder and you can hear the words from Preacher Alastair himself. Then the choice you have is to continue living this lie, or get out into the real world with the real people. I can't make that choice for you."

Alex set down the tape recorder and pressed play. All of the sisters moved closer to the tape. Alex stood over it.

Alastair's voice came out with the words My Sister was my First… his confession continued and Alex stayed over the tape recorder until such point she knew the crowd were listening. She had visions of Sister Teresa running forward to capture the tape recorder. Within minutes Sister Teresa disappeared. Alex slowly walked backwards and left the room. She didn't want to be there at the end of the tape as it was their discussion on what was to come next for them. She walked through the kitchen and back through the door she had entered a few hours ago. It was dark now and she could just about make out the part of the wall she had climbed over to get into the house. As she walked across the garden she couldn't help looking for the graves of the children, but she couldn't see them. Preacher Alastair had them tucked away fairly well in the corner of the garden.

Bang!

There was a large explosion noise. Alex recognised it as a gun shot just as she was clipped in the arm. It was only a flesh wound but the spin had her turned around and fallen on the floor. She could make out Sister Teresa from the house walking towards her, Shot gun, twelve bore, two bullets move were the words going through Alex's head. She rolled to the left just in time as the second shot hit the ground. She pulled her gun and fired directly at the sister. She hit the ground. Alex got up and she could see that the Sister was no longer holding the gun. She walked over towards her, Alex had managed to put four into her as she lay on the ground. By this time there were faces at the window although none came out. Alex assessed the bullet wounds. Two in the leg one in the arm and one just below her belly button.

"You couldn't just leave us alone could you?"

"Leave you alone after what you have done to these poor women? You are as bad as the preacher. You helped lure in his prey and covered up for him when he needed it." Alex was now standing directly over her.

"I loved him, he was a great man. A man of god."

"Then you are as crazy as he was."

"This isn't the end. You can't stop what we have built here. God is looking over us and what you have done to Preacher Alastair that will just make him stronger at the hand of our lord. This isn't the end!"

Alex stopped and thought about that. She believed her, through what she had seen and heard today. These things just don't end. Sister Teresa's injuries weren't going to kill her. By the time an ambulance arrives on site she will have spun a story to these women about how the devil got in, how she fought it and it ran, how we must be together even more now, probably even find a new male to keep the conception going. Sister Teresa was right these things never end. Alex lifted her gun again. This probably wasn't the end of the cult, but it was going to end for Sister Teresa. Alex ensured the fifth bullet was going to end her life. Straight between her eyes.

There were still faces at the window as Alex turned back towards the garden. It took a couple of minutes but she found the place on the wall where she had climbed over, as she climbed and sat at the top she took one look back, she could just about make out a few people standing around Sister Teresa. By the time she was over the wall she had convinced herself that the women were kicking the dead body of the sister on the floor. It made her feel happier about leaving them to fend for themselves.

Alex stood on the other side of the wall, a black Mercedes was parked within six feet. Alex climbed into the back seat.

"Did the camera stay down?"

The man in the driver's seat closed the laptop he was holding and placed it on the seat next to him.

"Yes Alex, did it all go as planned. Is it dealt with?"

"Yes, as well as I could have hoped for."

Oliver, Mr Mellor's personal pilot turned around to see Alex holding her shoulder.

"What happened to you are you okay?"

"I am fine it's just a flesh wound we can sort it when we get to the hotel."

"Are you sure?"

"Yes its fine, let's go you know what the traffic is like."

Oliver turned and started the car. They drove straight on for an hour or so, and then as they did, they could see the sky line of New York in front of them.

Chapter Three

The Waldorf Astoria on Park Avenue was the perfect location for Alex to stay whilst in New York. Grand Central station was five blocks away, and if she needed to get lost in a crowd she could be in Times Square in under ten minutes by foot. Access for getting out of the city was three blocks away, the Queens midtown tunnel which lead onto the Long Island express way. A cab could be hailed in New York in seconds. Alex was conscious that something could change at any moment.

One of the most comforting factors was that she knew, it wasn't going to be the international police that were coming looking for her. She had managed to clear up the mess in Germany and England before arriving back home to the USA.

Alex had sat at Dr Smith's desk staring at the black case with the tracker devices glowing at her. The exact same one she had seen back at the apartment with Christopher Mellor. Her first thought had been to confront him, he knew more than he had told her, and now so did Alex. Well at least she believed she did. It had taken about ten minutes after the phone call to him for Alex to start to be concerned with what she had done. Inviting him to Germany had been a mistake. If Christopher Mellor, the multi billionaire had started the Brown Institute. He had pumped billions of dollars into this and he has been known to cover up murders. If Christopher Mellor was in fact, the person in charge here. What was he going to do with someone who could expose him and his family? Alex had just killed his only son in cold blood and what could possibly be his business partner. Although it was Michael who had killed his business partner's daughter Alana, all of this could be laid at her door.

No, calling him had been a mistake. She was going to need to control this situation with Christopher or there would be a good chance that she would disappear too.

Firstly. she needed the black case. This was a location of every murderer on Jack's list. The trouble was it was activated by a finger print. She was going to need Dr Smith's fingerprints every time she wanted to track or search for someone. There was a thought for a moment of chopping off his finger and carrying it around with her. This wasn't practical it was going to get rotten fast so she needed to try to see if a fingerprint on paper could trick the scanner. She walked out of the study and into the kitchen. Found a sponge and some food dye and proceeded to take Jonathan Smiths finger print. It didn't work. The red colouring wasn't strong enough. The print on the paper was too washy and smudged

In the office Alex had noticed a printer attached to the PC she took out the ink cartridge and broke it on the table. The powdered contents inside made a much darker print and after the third attempt the print was accepted. Alex started to feel and think like a criminal. Alex knew that one copy was not enough, lose that and I have lost everything. She made a dozen separate copies of Dr Smith's Finger print, and tested each in turn.

The Doctor's Computer was still open. In her bag she bought from the taxi she still had Jacks hard drive, there was no point trying to read everything that was on the PC. At the time she didn't know how long she had before the scene was discovered, so she needed to wrap this up as soon as possible.

Alex downloaded everything from the computer onto the hard drive. There were giga bytes of files and the process had taken nearly fifteen minutes to complete. Alex had spent a further twenty minutes sitting back in Dr Smith's chair trying to figure out a plan for the events of that evening. Alana had been shot with her police issued gun that Michael had stolen from the cabin when he killed Michael Simpson.

Michael Mellor and Dr Smith had both been shot with the unregistered gun that Mr Mellor's pilot Oliver had given to her. Alex would have to stage the scene to distract the police from the thought of a fourth person in this.

Her plan had Alana interrupting Michael breaking into the Doctor's computer, if the German police uncover Michael was born in the institute it could be as simple as that. He wanted to know where he came from and how.

The Doctor's computer would show that files had been downloaded. Alex planted a USB flash drive into the terminal and download the same as she had on her hard drive. The capacity wasn't the same but she left the PC with a message on the screen stating not enough room on device. That would have been because Michael was interrupted.

Alana shoots at Michael and misses thinking him an intruder. Alex walked over to the door and shot directly at the wall.

Michael returns fire and kills Alana, Dr Smith hears the gun shot runs down stairs and after words and tears, grabs the gun Alana had, and shoots Michael. This meant that Alana and Michael could stay pretty much where they were, with no need to touch the bodies again.

Doctor Smith however needed to look like he had committed suicide. Remorse for what he had done, and for the loss of his only daughter. It was the only cover up Alex could come up with. Unfortunately, Alex had stood over him and shot him directly in the head. The suicide somehow needed to blow a whole big enough in his head that it covered up the first bullet hole.

Alex searched the house for a further fifteen minutes. She had been getting more and more worried the longer she spent in the house that someone was going to discover them. Finally, she found a shot gun the ideal thing. Lifting Doctor Smith's body onto the chair in front of the computer Alex placed the shotgun in his mouth, she climbed almost underneath the desk to ensure gun powder residue was on his hands, she pulled the trigger, the noise was loud and the spray covered Alex even from where she was.

It had done a good job, hiding the first bullet wound. The doctor's skull had exploded taking almost the front of his face off. Alex just hoped that the medical examiner didn't look too closely to the events of the evening. Chris Masters back in the US, he would have spotted what she had done, she was sure of it. Alex left them in those positions, took the black case with the tracking device in and the hard drive and went to the kitchen. She washed up and the cleaned down the surfaces as much as possible and then left the house. She had been half way down the drive before she remembered the ink and the finger prints. She ran back into the house and cleaned that up also. Taking time to ensure that she cleaned the doctor's fingers. Alex carried her stuff out the main drive and walked for about a mile before hailing a cab. She didn't want to be picked up close to the murder scene. She then went back to the hotel. Once she was safely back in her room she called Mr Mellor from the hotel telling him not to come. Alex wasn't worried that he had dropped everything for her. She needed to clear her name with the police in England and return to the US, they would speak then.

Alex explained to Christopher Mellor she had taken care of the scene at Jonathan Smiths house and there was nothing to lead them back to him or her. Mr Mellor hadn't spoken in return. One of his men had held the phone to his ear, she knew he was listening. The first call a few hours ago Alex had explained to him "I know everything." She didn't, but she hoped that the information she had just downloaded was going to give her everything.

Alex also explained on the phone that she was going to need Maria to collaborate with her story, she told him what Maria was going to have to collaborate with and trusted him to get it sorted. There had still been no response other than the man holding the phone telling Alex everything had been understood. Then the phone was dead.

The next morning Alex went to the airport and got the pilot to take her back to the UK. There was a doubt that when she got on the plane whether he would or not. He was Mr Mellor's employee. Alex didn't have a gun to threaten him with, but he didn't know that. She had, had to leave her weapon at the crime scene. Over hearing the pilot speaking to the tower making arrangements for a flight to London Luton Airport had put her at ease. The flight was going in the correct direction.

On arrival, Alex presented herself into the police at the airport before arriving through customs. She had been taken to the local station where about three hours later a team of detectives turned up to question her about the past seven days. They had been looking into her movements and she needed to explain herself.

Alex took them back to the Deacon James case in America. Everyone in the world had heard about that by now. She explained that the captain had given her two weeks off to recuperate. Maria Mellor had heard about this. Due to the fact that Alex had recently saved her brother's life in a night club. She sent her tickets for a break in Rome and flights and everything. She thought why not. Why not take the break? She packed up that day and headed to Italy. To her surprise Maria was there in Italy also. She had presumed it was just a gift. There was a note in her hotel room asking to meet her at the colosseum at eight p.m. signed M. Alex took in some sites and then went to meet Maria. The guard had told her that it was a private tour, she knew the Mellor's were super rich so she thought nothing more of it. To her further surprise Maria wasn't there Michael Mellor was. Michael then confessed everything.

He confessed that he had attacked the boy in the nightclub not the other way around, and it hadn't been his first. He had assaulted quite a few people even stabbed a couple of them. He just wanted to look at their face whilst they bled in front of him. Michael had confessed his need to murder someone and it felt to Alex, this was the sole reason she was there. She was going to be his victim. How ever Michael had somehow become delusional about the fact that Alex had taken away a murder victim from him. The altercation she interrupted in the nightclub was destined to be his first kill. In Michaels mind Alex needed to pay, he had lost someone that was special to him. His first kill. Michael's fantasy hadn't been to kill Alex but to ensure she lost someone close to her.

Alex then discovered that Michael had Alex followed since the incident in the club. He knew she had slept with Michael the brother of her ex-partner Paul and as such he somehow thought that he was the one to pay.

Alex had tried to reason with Michael but he wasn't listening. She pointed out to the police that she didn't even see him face to face. Explaining that Michael had placed the speakers on the ground and that they could check with the coliseum guards as they must have been the ones to clean them up afterwards.

Alex had ran out of the colosseum and headed back to the hotel to get word to Michael Simpson, but was attacked on the steps up to the main road. By whom she could only believe was Michael Mellor. He stole her gun. She had gone back to the hotel dizzy and slightly concussed. She ended up passing out on the bed before she could contact anyone. During the night Michael had tried to attack her again but the night porter interrupted. The hotel kindly then moved her to another room. Again they could check this out with the hotel. The morning came and all she had wanted to do was go home. But she was worried what Michael was going to do with a gun. She tried calling Michaels father who she had met recently to no prevail. Then tried calling Maria, Michael's sister. Maria was distraught and she was actually in Italy also. She had travelled with her brother and planned to take her to lunch that day to thank her, she knew nothing of the meeting with Michael.

Alex went to visit her at her home and when she arrived she discovered that Michael had called Maria saying he was heading to England. He had taken a commercial flight as to leave the plane with Maria so she could get home. Maria gave the plane to Alex to follow Michael and stop him before he did anything illegal.

Alex then followed Michael to the UK. Having only ever been here once before she didn't really know where to start. She knew where Michael's parents lived. Well the village anyway. She went there and asked for directions… The Five Bells pub if she had remembered they could check with the barmaid. Tall dark hair spoke with a foreign accent. She gave Alex the directions to Michael's parent's house but there was no answer she tried around the back but still no answer. After five minutes she left. After leaving she had remembered that Michael lived somewhere near some stone cows so she Googled England stone cows and it comes up on Wikipedia Milton Keynes. She booked into a Milton Keynes hotel and thought she would go looking for him in the morning. She had been trying Michaels phone but to no joy, and by now she was exhausted from the last forty-eight hours.

The morning came and she searched for Michael everywhere she couldn't find him. At this point she was getting even more worried. She had phoned his work, his cell phone, his parents' house. She went to his home. Michael's work had given her the address but nobody was there. She had slept that night outside his house hoping he would return. It was the phone that woke her in the morning. Maria had taken a call from Michael and he was heading to Germany. Whilst she didn't want to leave the country without speaking to Michael Simpson. She also half wondered if that was were Michael was and so Michael Mellor had been following him, she needed to capture Michael Mellor so she got back on the plane that she had left in Luton. Maria had arranged for the pilot to wait and bring them back to Italy if possible. She went to the hotel that Maria had suggested. Michael Mellor had been to Germany a few times before with the family and they always stayed at the same place, but he was not there. He had checked in but not been seen. She waited in reception for any sign of him and that is where she saw the news. She was shocked to say the least about Michael's parents. She knew Michael Mellor had done this and he was more dangerous than they had expected so she came back to England to clear this up and also to get some help in capturing Michael.

It was a credible story and one that had milestones in order for the police to check it out. Alex was placed in a holding cell, and everyone disappeared to follow through on her story. In that cell Michael Simpson had played on her mind, she knew Michael's body was back at the cabin. He deserved better than this. She hadn't told anyone and she couldn't as she would be incriminating her own story.

Michael had said on their trip down there that the cabin hadn't been used in years. So maybe when they find him it will have been enough time for them to just chalk it up to Michael Mellor. Alex was fed and made comfortable as she was going to be there overnight whilst they checked out her story. By the morning the police had called her back into the interview room. Thanked her for her assistance and asked if she needed help getting back to the states. They had checked out her story with Maria Mellor, Christopher Mellor, her captain back in the US. The pilot had also given a statement as he was still at the airport awaiting her return. They also informed her that they had found Michael Mellor. He had broken into a house in Germany and it would seem shot a young girl. The girl's father had returned and shot Michael and then himself. There was no need to continue looking for him. Alex was relieved to hear that her plan had worked. That the German police had bought the whole murder suicide scene she had left for them.

She was told that they would also keep in contact with her for when they find Michael Simpson as he is still missing. If she did hear from him to let them know also.

Alex knew she wasn't going to hear from him, she knew where Michael was and just needed to get herself out of there. She thanked them and headed back to the airport. The journey back to the states had been one of investigation. She plugged in the hard drive and started to go through all the files off of Dr Smith's computer. There were thousands of documents for her to go through. Given it was a ten hour flight back home she had some time. Enough time to know that Christopher Mellor was heavily involved in the Institute. She had arranged to land at Newark airport. She didn't want to return directly to the Mellor's estate. She was going to need leverage before her first meeting with him.

At Newark airport she took the hard drive, laptop tracking device and the finger prints and headed to the nearest PC store. She made ten copies of the hard drive and the finger prints, and set about storing them in different locations.

In Grand Central Station she had left three copies of the hard drive and finger sprints in different lockers. She returned to Newark airport and JFK and placed copies in lockers there. She mailed a copy to her brother, and another to her father with the clear instructions not to download the hard drive enclosed or open the envelopes unless something had happened to her.

Alex also had stated she would be in contact soon. Something today she still hadn't done. It played at the back of her mind now as she knew they were worried. She kept two copies for herself and she intended to hand a copy over to Christopher Mellor as proof to what she had discovered. Although she didn't really understand it herself yet. The thought that she did was going to be enough hopefully to put some doubt into Christopher Mellor's mind especially if he was as corrupt as she thought he was.

When it had been time to call Christopher, Alex had had butterflies. Everything she was learning about this guy was that he wasn't a guy that you should be looking to blackmail. That is exactly what Alex wanted to do. She had started on a journey that she needed to finish and she was going to need him to play his part in this process.

The meeting had gone so much better than expected. Alex had arranged it to be in the Waldorf Astoria for the same reasons she was still staying there. Plus, the fact that it was a public place. She had been cleared by the police and she had already mentioned her involvement with the Mellor's so there would be no reason for them not to meet.

Christopher came with his bodyguard team which had been a little intimidating for Alex but she had stayed strong. Alex had told him she had twelve different cloud accounts where she had placed this information also with time locked emails that unless she logged in within twenty four hours, emails and the information would be released worldwide. There were hard copies of what she handed over strategically placed across New York with links to cloud accounts so that they can be retrieved. Alex pointed out that she had all the bases covered.

Christopher didn't doubt any of this, she had become a very resourceful person. Infact he was far to calm for Alex's liking.

She laid out her terms. Firstly, she wanted the Brown Institute closed down, the research they were doing needed to stop. Mr Mellor didn't flinch and just agreed. Alex thought about this later. He didn't need to close anything down as she would never know if he did or he didn't. Perhaps it was why it didn't faze him as much as she had hoped.

She wanted unlimited resources to carry on her quest for these murderers. He handed over a black card. The same one that Maria and Michael had. These were reserved for the worlds very rich, and Christopher Mellor had a spare. He pointed out there is no pin and it had already been registered to her. It was as if he had expected her to ask for money. This had been too easy. He was rolling over on everything. She had tried to push him. She asked for the plane. And then the pilot. She got both things and Christopher Mellor pointed out to her that his pilot was more than just a pilot. He had been ex British SAS the greatest fighting force in the world, majoring in electronics and hand to hand combat. If she was going to use him then she should really be using him. The meeting had ended and Christopher left as if it was just another meeting. He shook Alex's hand and wished her luck on her quest, and if she was to need anything more? Just call him.

Alex had killed his son and blackmailed him into unlimited funds and resources. She knew deep down it wouldn't be as simple as that.

Chapter Four

Alex collected her key from reception and headed straight for her suite. The card that Christopher had given to her almost demanded the best of the best. Oliver was in the suite next door. She had been in the states for three months now. Solved, in Alex's mind over fourteen cases. None of the murderers were still alive to tell their story but Alex had done her job by taking them off the streets. Oliver had shown to become more and more resourceful. Everything she asked of him so far he was able to do. Like cutting feeds to cameras, electronic gates all of it, he was as resourceful as she was.

Washington and New York was filled with children from the Brown Institute. It was like she had discovered in the early days of her research. There were pockets of these children all over the world.

Recommendations to the foundation means that you must know the people you are recommending, so they are either family or they are at least close friends to you. This meant that children of the institute stayed close to each other. Alex had taken down the top fourteen so far with self-confessed preacher Alistair Lee being number fourteen.

There was only one other serious case in the area that needed resolving, then she was planning a return home. Under the radar of her Captain and work colleagues but Alex wanted to see her family to make sure they were ok and for them to know that she was. She had no intention of going back to work. Not until this job was done.

Alex unlocked the door to her suite and went in. she threw her bag on the bed and headed for the shower. The thought of Alastair Lee and all those women made her skin crawl. She stood under the shower for a while, remembering how she used to smell the blood. How she would, at the beginning of this quest be taking three showers a day to try and get rid of the smell. Surprised now how it doesn't faze her at all. She finished showering and ordered room service. They had been in the hotel suite for over seven weeks and she was yet to visit the restaurant or share a meal with Oliver.

Room service arrived and when the waiter had disappeared, Alex went over to the desk that was in the corner and pulled a file from the draw. It was Stephen Henderson. Stephen Henderson was born in the Brown Institute back in 1992, to his parents Sophia and Robert Henderson. Robert Henderson was now the Secretary of State. This was going to be an issue. Alex had become very familiar with the tracking device and Stephen had been in the vicinity of the two girls attacked in central Park a fortnight ago and again last week where one was raped and killed. No witness's and the police had nothing to go on.

Alex could tell that Stephen was spiralling out of control. Her first thought had been to go after him before Alastair but this was going to be tricky for her. Stephen would have security, not just security but secret service security. Clearly he knew how to skip past them for what he had been doing. This gave Alex hope she could get close to him. Stephen had only been in New York for less than two months, this was after a much public fall out with his father. Deciding to move from Washington and start a life on his own. She read through his file, everything was normal. Well, normal for a Brown Institute baby. The only thing that troubled her was the recommendation on his file. This had changed to just say The Board. The board had recommended them to the institute.

Every other file she had read to this point someone, or a couple had made the recommendations but this one was just The Board.

There was no telling when Stephen would strike again, although it had been a week since the murder. Alex knew that once he had tasted the kill, there was something that would be pulling him back to it. Tonight was not going to be the night though. Stephen had been called back to Washington for a family meal at the Whitehouse. There had been a visiting dignity from the middle-east and they liked to show family union at these functions. Something he hadn't refused. Although he was living in New York alone, his father's credit cards were still footing the bill. Alex knew he would be watched tonight. Given his age and no doubt a petulant meeting with his father, Stephen's craving after tonight was going to be strong. Alex was almost sure that tomorrow night something was going to happen.

The club sandwich and fries had filled a gap, and she had almost become customary to the small bottles of wine in the fridge. Although the hotel must know her by now as they are stocking five to six new bottles in there every day.

Alex grabbed a couple bottles of wine and laid on the bed. Reruns of Magnum PI were playing on the TV but not that she was watching them. Alex was thinking hard what to do about Stephen Henderson. Something in her head said leave this one alone. He will be dealt with by his own people at some point, he isn't going to be able to escape them forever. That wasn't Alex's style, at some point someone is going to deal with him… but is that two, three or five more girls in the ground before that happens.

No, Alex knew who he was, and what he had done, the someone? Who was going to deal with him? That someone was her.

She needed to log on before sleep took her. She pulled a laptop out of the side draw of the bed and logged onto the hotels internet. She hadn't been bluffing Christopher Mellor when she told him she made copies of the file and uploaded them. The guy in the PC store had set up her cloud accounts for her, she had handed over a wedge of the money from the safe on the plane so no questions had been asked. Logging onto each account one by one, Alex changed the date of the outgoing email to tomorrow. She paused half way through them and started again.

Changing each date to the day after tomorrow. Tomorrow night she was hopeful of dealing with Stephen. If things had gone wrong and she was captured or worse? Then another day before the world knew about Christopher Mellor hadn't been too much bad of thing.

Sleep had become so much easier over the last two months. Michael Mellor was gone. Nobody was looking for her and she was living in luxury. Her new day job had been somewhat dangerous but the element of surprise she had, always worked in her favour. Nobody was expecting Alex when she turned up.

It was morning before she knew it. And later than expected, it was nine a.m. when Alex awoke. Placing a call, her breakfast was delivered. After breakfast she rang Oliver's room. He answered straight away. It was almost like he had been waiting at the end of the phone for the call. Oliver met with Alex in the reception area of the hotel. Stephens's apartment was close to Maddison Square Gardens it was a ten minute walk west of the hotel. The idea was to stake it out to know if he had been returning. There were a few coffee shops in distance of the apartment so they could sit and watch. It was one p.m. before Stephen showed up back to his apartment accompanied by two Secret Service officials.

The couple of hours they had sat and watched had been mostly in silence. Oliver worked away on his laptop and Alex sat and read the paper. It had been the times newspaper and she had been sitting looking through each of the articles. There were crimes and misdemeanours a plenty. All the activities that Alex had been involved in had hit the news. Nobody as yet had tied them all together. Alex suspected the police had but they weren't going to release that information. Bad guys dying was one thing. A vigilante on the loose would be something else to explain.

Now Stephen was back in New York and if Alex's feelings were correct he would be out to take his frustration out on someone this evening. Alex asked Oliver to find her a stun gun. She had an idea to trap Stephen in the park, much the same plan as she had back in her early police days. The night she first kissed Chris Masters. Alex would wander in the dark places in the park with the hope of attracting some attention.

Taking the short walk over to *Macys* Alex picked up some appropriate clothing for this evenings work. Walking through the department store she realised she had unlimited funds, and here she was in the shopping mecca of New York. Yet all she could think about was how does she capture Stephen Henderson's attention. Alex bought a suitable outfit and returned to the hotel.

Oliver had sourced the stun gun and returned to the coffee shop, he spent the afternoon watching the apartment. Nothing had happened since they arrived. Alex spent the afternoon in her room. Working on the files and the tracker. Alex knew that she was heading to see her parents next. There were one or two people in the neighbourhood that could be dealt with at the same time. There was no point wasting the trip, if she got the opportunity to clean up a couple of other cases.

The beauty of the tracking device they had implanted in the Brown Institute children was that it was always recording. Alex could find the time of a crime and put it into the tracker and bingo if it was one of her special Brown Institute babies then she was able to pin point who it was and where they were now.

Alex had thought about handing this device over a lot. This was going to help the police no end. Her fear now was that then they would look deeper into her and what she had been doing.

Her kill rate was higher than twenty now. Not including the murder of Sophie, the innocent mother of what would have sure to become a psychopathic son.

No if she handed it in then she may as well go directly to jail herself. Not everyone was going to understand this. This was her quest and for now, she needed to operate above the law.

The NY Knicks were playing the Dallas Cowboys tonight at the gardens, Alex took the bet that Stephen would be going as he was a huge fan. She bought two tickets for her and Oliver on the court so she could see all around the stadium. Dressed to kill and Oliver at her side they went to the game. After purchasing some drinks and a big foam finger just to fit in, they headed courtside. Stephen was already seated not ten feet from her.

Stephen and Oliver both sat and got engrossed in the game. Alex watched Stephen and the two body guards that were sitting just behind him. First three quarters of the game went with no hiccups the guards had fetched him beer and food and they all sat enjoying the game.

In the last minute of the fourth quarter, Stephen got up to leave. The guards behind him rose also. Then sat back down. Alex had presumed that he had told them he was just going to the bathroom, just there. As he pointed over to the door just off the floor. Stephen walked away from the guards and headed towards the bathroom. Alex and Oliver knew at this point he wasn't going to be coming back so he needed to be followed. Stephen had taken a look back to see both security guys looking directly at him and then pushed the door and went into the toilet. Oliver followed him in. There was no way out of the bathroom. He stood and washed his hands as Stephen waited around. It was as if he was waiting for a sign. He was. The end of the game had been the sign as soon as the buzzer went so did Stephen. His bodyguards weren't going to be able to follow him and the other forty thousand people leaving at the same time. What Stephen didn't know was that Alex and Oliver were very close on his tail. He had shaken off his guards and headed out of the building. Heading past Macys and towards Times Square. Stephen knew anyone could get lost in the tourists in Times Square. Before the main square he turned Left and went into D&Bs sports bar. Up the escalators and into the bar. His bodyguards were going to be spending a while looking through all the streets. Stephen was gone and out of site.

Stephen stood at the bar and drank, beer followed by a whiskey chaser. Alex counted at least five before she knew it was time for her to leave. Oliver was to wait with him in the bar and Alex was to go on ahead to the park. He wasn't going to be able to drink much more before his appetite took over. He would want to be semi functional for the activity ahead.

Alex needed to be there ahead of Stephen so that she could at least let him stalk her for a bit. Alex walked through Times Square and down to the park. She aimed for the centre, under the bridge and down by the fountain as good as a place to be seen at first. It was a common meeting place in the park and accessible from each side. Alex sat on the wall with phone in hand waiting for a text from Oliver to say that they had left the bar.

"Looking for company love?"

Alex hadn't even seen the guy approach. He was a middle aged guy. In what seemed to be a very worn out suit.

"Sorry?"

"Looking for company? You know for the evening?"

Alex was a bit thrown with the conversation. Her mind had been focused on Stephen.

"Sorry?" She then got what he had been saying. The guy had thought Alex was a hooker looking for business.

"No! I am not a prostitute."

"Okay love, are you sure?" The man was a little taken back by Alex's tone.

"Yes I am sure. Now jog on," Alex pulled out her police badge and the guy walked on. She was back to looking at her phone. Stephen had left the bar and was heading through Times Square in her direction.

She kept the phone in her hand until the point that Oliver had texted he is all yours. Oliver hadn't assisted Alex in any of the cases they had been on together, other than getting her and the person in the same vicinity. And taking care of any equipment or IT needs. This was her quest not his, he had his orders from Christopher Mellor to assist but not to be involved.

Alex hadn't asked him to either. She had kept the relationship strictly professional.

Alex paced up and down by the fountain. As if waiting for someone. She kept looking around her in all directions of the park suddenly she could see Stephen out of the corner of her eye. He was hooked, a little way off and in the shadows but he was watching her.

Alex walked under the tunnel and up the steps looked around and came back down again. There were several other people walking dogs and running through the park so she knew she was still safe at the moment. She pulled her phone out as if to look for messages but nothing.

Alex stormed off to the east end of the park. She knew that there were more deserted areas of the park there. She didn't look behind her as she didn't want to spook Stephen as he was bound to come up on her. She carried on walking, it seemed like it had taken forever for him to make his move. But then he did.

"Excuse me," Alex hadn't expected a conversation. She was adamant that he was just going to spring on her.

"Hi," Alex turned to see Stephen standing in front of her.

"Are you lost, do you need help out of the Park?"

"No I am fine, Thank you."

Alex turned again and headed on through the park.

"Wait, sorry was you waiting for someone?"

Alex turned her head back, but carried on walking as if trying to get away.

"Yes but I was stood up."

Alex just carried on walking.

"I can't believe that, good looking girl like you?"

Alex was thrown off. He was trying to chat her up. He definitely had the look of a Brown Institute baby, blonde hair six foot quite athletic. A good looking guy if she had ever seen one. This made Alex stop in her tracks.

"That's what I thought?"

"Can I buy you a coffee or something to ease the pain?"

Now Alex was stumped. If she said yes, were they actually going to go for coffee? If she said no was he just going to move on?

"I am fine thankyou."

Alex turned. It had been the right choice. No sooner had she turned his hands were upon her. Both shoulders, as she spun she pulled the stun gun and hit him square in the ribs. Stephen went to the ground hard. Within seconds he was out cold. Alex grabbed him and pulled him into the bushes. Flipping him over Alex cable tied his hands together and then waited for him to come around. It took about ten minutes for that to happen. Constantly surveying the area Alex came out of the bushes whilst waiting for him to ensure that nobody else in the park would have seen what just happened.

"How many?"

"How many what?" Stephen had started to play a familiar game for Alex.

"How many have you killed Stephen? Just like the girl last week and the attack on the two girls the week before. How many others have there been that we don't know about?"

Alex had her gun firmly pointed at Stephen. He knew she wasn't messing around.

"I am the Secretary of State's son, and my security are just behind me."

"No they are not Stephen, you lost them at the gardens after the game. But you didn't lose me. I followed you to D&B's sports bar and then to here." Stephen was trying to fathom that in his head.

"But you were already here?"

"I know Stephen, I was that confident in your actions that I left just before your sixth and final drink. I know you and you are a creature of habit, it's in your nature."

Stephen was worried. He thought he had been stalking Alex not the other way around.

"I haven't killed anyone? I don't know what you are talking about?"

"You're lying… Stephen you have a tracking device fitted under your skin that tells me where you are and what you have been doing. I can trace you here for the last couple of weeks and especially after you raped and killed that young girl… I know you Stephen… I know what you are. I know where you were born."

"What, no you don't. I am not being tracked, my father wouldn't allow it. You don't know where I was born I only found out a few months ago so there is no way."

"The Brown Institute in Paris."

Stephen was quiet. He had only just found out himself, that was part of the break up with his father. He hadn't told him until now. Someone in the media had been asking questions about his father and mothers relationship. He had been forty-two and his wife twenty-two when they had Stephen. The press had found out about the IVF treatment and his father needed to tell him before it was released.

"How do you know?"

"I know everything Stephen that's why I know you have been doing this type of thing before."

"I haven't."

Alex stood over Stephen for a while looking directly at him. She only knew the events of the last few weeks. Alex had read enough cases to know that these feelings don't come up overnight.

"I have all night Stephen."

"What are you going to do to me? You know who I am? You know my father is going to come after you if you do anything to me."

Alex did know who he was and that was still worrying her. She was already convinced by now that the local police would be tying things together but she didn't need the FBI, Secret Service and the force of the government looking for her.

"How many Stephen, just answer the question?"

Stephen took a moment to answer.

"No more, I told you the truth. I haven't killed another person. I have attacked a few but it's never gone as far as it did last week. I didn't mean to kill her, things just got well out of hand and the next thing I knew she wasn't moving. There was a girl at my prom and a few after that and as you said a few two weeks ago. I have tried to stop myself. I even told my father what happened last week and that we should go to the police. He was mad but he said he would take care of it. You should have heard the righteous bastard last night. He just went on and on about what a disappointment I was and what he had to sacrifice for me. For me, he has done nothing. He chose to go into office, with these security guys and in the eyes of the public not me."

Alex had hoped that someone else was going to deal with him. It was evident now that they were not. They are going to cover his tracks in the first murder and how many more would he be able to get away with? Alex walked over towards him and placed the gun on his forehead.

"Swear to me you are telling the truth."

"It's the truth I swear." Stephen was almost in tears.

Alex put the gun down. She tore open his shirt and took a pen out of her pocket she wrote in big black letters on his chest. *I killed Andrea Stevens last week and I told my dad.*

"What are you doing?"

"People need to know what you have done Stephen, if your father is going to cover this up then I am not. The world needs to know what you are and stop you."

"We can give you money. My father is loaded he will make sure that you are taken care of. If you just let me go."

"I don't need money Stephen, I am as rich as I need to be."

Alex looked directly at him leaning against the tree. Unsure what her next move needed to be.

She decided to drag him closer to the main path way so at least someone was going to discover him. She placed him virtually in the middle of the path. She leant over him with the gun and looked him square in the eye without saying a word. She paused for a moment as if frozen. Lifted her arm and knocked Stephen unconscious on the ground. She took out her phone and took a picture of him as he laid there. She was going to let him live. It was so much against her desire, but she needed someone to know what he had done and it would hurt him more to go to prison. And his father for covering this up.

Alex sent the photo to one of her cloud accounts and then turned to walk away. As she did, the thought of the murder, the thought of the women who had been attacked, what they had gone through came rushing back to her. She was letting him get away with what he had done. She couldn't live with that she couldn't live with the thought of him doing that to those women. Sure he had only killed one but how many of these women were now living in fear because he had attacked them. That thought was too strong for Alex. She turned and ran back to the body. Stephen was still lying unconscious on the ground she pulled out her gun and stood above him. She hadn't killed anyone who she wasn't face to face with before, she thought about trying to revive him in order to kill him whilst looking him in the eyes but that might take too long. No, Stephen Henderson deserved it. He was as bad as the rest of them and now he had the power of the government behind him. They were going to cover up everything that he was doing. She stood over Stephen's unconscious body and took aim.

The pain in the side of her head didn't last long. It was sharp and fast and she was unconscious before she hit the ground.

Chapter Five

Alex awoke slowly and opened her eyes, she could make out the sound of people talking around her. By the time her focus returned she could tell she was back in her hotel suite in the Waldorf Astoria.

"Boss," she heard a man's voice from the corner of the room but she was still a bit groggy.

Before she knew it, Christopher Mellor was passing her a glass of water.

"How are you feeling Alex?"

"Fine, I think? What happened?"

"All in good time Alex, but your head okay? Take your time I know some of my guys aren't as gentle as I would like them to be."

Alex was processing that through her head again before replying. Her focus and her mind became a lot sharper as the adrenaline kicked in.

"You hit me?"

"No, technically James hit you, but Alex you need to understand some things. There are rules to what we are doing here."

"Wait, you knocked me out in the park. What happened to Stephen Henderson?"

By now Alex was trying to find her feet.

"Alex sit down, sit down!" from the tone of Christopher's voice she knew he meant it.

"Alex, I have been very reasonable have I not? We have either met all your demands or currently working towards them. In return for my agreement and generosity we need to set some ground rules down before we go any further."

"What happened to Stephen?"

"Alex, I will get to that I promise you. As for now, I need you to listen to me. Okay. Listen, which means sitting down and calming down." Christopher had a serious expression on his face, one that Alex knew to obey.

"What has happened with Stephen Henderson is not to be repeated to anyone. Are we clear? What he has done and what you have done this evening will be forgotten. He will be dealt with but by his parents and his people, we are not to get involved."

"He is a killer."

"Alex I said listen not reply. We know what he is, and we know what he has done. And he will be dealt with, accordingly. There are bigger things at stake here Alex than his little misdemeanour in the park the other night."

Alex's blood started to boil. His misdemeanour cost a girl her life.

"I know how this must make you feel. But listen to what I am saying Alex, Stephen Henderson is off limits."

Alex heard him. Although her mind was set that Stephen was a problem that she needed to solve.

"I understand what you are saying, it doesn't make it right he is a killer."

"Good, I am glad you understand," Christopher was ignoring the second comment.

"Can I ask a question?"

Christopher knew she wouldn't lay down as simple as that.

"Yes as long as you know it may not be the answer you like."

"Okay, what happened with Stephen?"

Christopher paused before telling her.

"He has been returned to his father. Before you check yes we took the picture off your phone and closed the cloud account that you sent it too. Alex you must have known that Stephen was a bridge to far even for you? Given what we are trying to achieve here. Together we are attempting to clean up this mess. You must know that having the Secret Service looking for you is not a good idea? Hell, how you have distracted Interpol was a stroke of genius, but don't push your luck."

Christopher was being more supportive now. Alex did know that she shouldn't have pursued it. She had her own doubts in the matter. But the thought of another murderer getting away with it was more that she could bare. Alex was clouded by that thought so much she couldn't think clearly enough about the outcome.

"What about Oliver?"

"He is fine. He is next door in his suite. You know he is becoming over protective of you… almost took James' head off when he heard what we had done."

Alex sat back in her chair. There was no more to get out of this. Christopher had covered up in some form what Stephen had done. Either to protect himself, what they were doing, or her, or maybe even Stephen, she wasn't really sure.

It was a relief Oliver wasn't part of this, she had come to trust him a lot and the thought of him still working alongside Christopher had been one she had toyed with over the past two months. Alex's trust was hard to give but once she did, she gave it fully.

"So, Alex I think we have an understanding, yes? Maybe New York and Washington have seen enough of our justice for a while. There are plenty more states for you to be working through."

Alex just nodded back at Christopher. He was right in the fact that there were lots of other Brown Institute children out there. Although Alex didn't like the taste of leaving one alone.

"How is everything else then Alex? I have been following your progress over the last couple of months with interest. Amazing some of the work you have been doing and some of the people you have been taking care of, I especially liked the priest, what was his name? I want to say William McPherson?"

Alex nodded again.

"Genius, to feed him his own testicles as well Alex, above and beyond the call of duty," Alex just stared back at Christopher.

She hadn't intended to do that; she had intended to stop his reign of terror but not in such a graphic way. The man had no remorse for his actions and when Alex had arrived at the church she believed him to be alone. She had followed Father William back from the soup kitchen that he worked in on a Thursday evening, back into the church and he headed back into his study. She spent ten minutes checking the church had been empty and the other doors were locked. Alex hadn't noticed the small door at the back of the study when she had been surveilling him over the past few days. When she came through the door for the study, Father William was not alone. There was a young altar boy, dressed as an altar boy although it was nearly nine p.m. A young boy, by the name of Jason Keynes he was barely ten years old and had snuck out of the house at the father's request.

Jason was on his knees in front of the father. Alex was shocked at the sight and almost shot father William there and then.

Father William didn't even flinch, he just requested that she let the little boy finish before they started. Alex ran over and pulled the boy away from the father. As she did William knocked her to the ground. Then turned his attention to Jason, stood straight over him and broke his neck in seconds. Alex was enraged. She managed to lift her leg and kick him in the place Jason had been paying attention too. The Father was on the floor in pain. There was no need for what he had done. He had been found out but he still wanted one more kill. Alex had picked him off the ground and placed him back in his chair. She punched him straight on the nose to ensure she had his attention. Father William proceeded to tell Alex if he was to be caught he wanted to feel it one more time. He almost gloated at the fact that this wasn't the first, it wasn't the fifth.

Young boys had disappeared where ever he was and there had been an underlying acceptance from the church that it had been him. There must have been as he was still practicing. Alex took her gun and placed it on his forehead. He muttered the number under his breath to her, he didn't want to say it out loud. He had taken eleven lives.

With his dying breath as a man of god did he want to repent his sins? Did he want to confess all to the man he had served? No, Father William thought his last words were going to be "I will miss the feeling of my balls in some boy's mouth." Alex wasn't about to let that happen.

She ordered him to strip. Which he did. She then took the letter opener of the Fathers desk and told him to cut off his own balls. She gave him the choice, it's either that father or the gun. The father started the job but passed out after the first cut. Alex finished the job and then placed them in his mouth. She had to wait over two hours before he awoke. He wasn't awake for long. Long enough for Alex to ask how it felt. Then Alex did really finish the job.

As she had with the others she amended her file and left it on the desk. Showing his known kills and now for the police to look for the others that he had confessed too. Alex was meticulous with the paperwork. It had all been printed fresh that morning so there were no finger prints on the paper and all in a sealed envelope so there was no

DNA. Being a policewoman, daughter and sister of a police man meant that she knew how to leave a crime scene.

"He wasn't a good father."

"I gathered that Alex, it was a fitting ending for him. Now I have business to attend. Is there anything else you need from me, Alex before we leave? I trust you have had no problem with the card or the situation. Although I must say you are very resourceful... Maria could spend the amount you have in two months on a shopping trip"

"No, things are okay," Alex just wanted him to leave.

"Good, now if you do need anything give me a call, Alex." Christopher nodded towards the door to his team. They assembled and left. Alex got off the chair and walked over to the bathroom. Her head was still a little fuzzy from the hit in the park last night. From the clock in the hall way it was six a.m., she must have been out for at least seven hours, and what's more Christopher must have been close. He must be following them. Alex needed to be more observant about who is around her.

She washed her face and felt for the lump on her head. It had been a good whack. Alex was still feeling the effects so she chose to take a lie down before she decided her next move. Before she did she wanted to ensure that Oliver was okay. She rang his room and as always he answered almost immediately.

"Hi."

"Hi, are you okay?"

"I am fine, Alex, are you?"

"Yes, a bit of a sore head, but everything is okay. Christopher was just pointing out he, we, didn't need the attention of the Secret Service. I suppose he is correct."

"I didn't know he was here. Do you need me to get anything for you?"

"No I am good. Just need a few hours' sleep. I will call you when I wake and we will decide what we are doing next."

"Okay, sleep well."

Alex put the phone down. For the first time since they had been together she had the feeling that she could have done with waking up with him. Just someone to put their arms around her to give her some comfort would have been a start. It wasn't long before she was asleep again, this time without the aid of the club to the back of the head.

When Alex awoke it was one p.m. She had slept longer than she expected to. She ordered room service and took a shower and packed a small bag. She had intentions of coming back to New York so she hadn't thought about checking out. This was a good a base as any to work from, especially when she had copies of everything in Grand Central Station and the airport. Room service arrived and she logged on and extended the times on her email accounts to tomorrow evening.

Alex phoned Oliver and as always he was waiting by the phone.

"We are going home. I need to see my parents and ensure that they are okay."

"Okay, I will bring the car."

Alex hung up and went down to reception to wait for him. Within minutes he had arrived and she sat in the back. It had become so customary she didn't know if she should change and ride up front with him.

"It's about two hours south of here."

"I know where you live Alex."

Alex wasn't shocked at this; she almost knew he would know. He was always a few steps ahead of her and very efficient. She sat back and started to go through the two files that she had relevant for her trip home. She knew whilst she was there she could cover these off before heading back to New York and then to Washington. Alex had listened to Christopher Mellor's warning, and didn't have any intentions in visiting Stephen Henderson but there were still a few in Washington that she needed to spend some quality time with.

Martin Bates was the first of the two files. Born to the institute in the early 80s in an out of prison over the last ten years for various offences including GBH, ABH and robbery with violence. Alex knew his crimes had escalated to a double murder robbery at a home not far from where her brother, Jason, lived. Not his usual MO so that's why he hadn't yet been connected to this. There had been another attempt three days later at a second home where the owner had over powered him but he got away. Alex wanted to stop him before he got any further.

The second was a more interesting case. This guy was working on becoming the next world famous serial killer. Craig Curle, he had been a recommendation from the Mellor's so Alex knew he had to come from money. This was a concern to her, she didn't know whether she was going to end up seeing Mr Mellor again if she went after him. Craig had been making a lot of noise about his killings. Alex convinced herself that if Mr Mellor had wanted her to keep away, he would have added the address to the places for her not to visit. There had been a spell of missing persons from the town. Nearly eight in total now, although four were so far recovered. Craig was escalating. The four recovered bodies had all been held for up to two weeks.

It had been very similar to a case she had read about in the UK. Where the killer liked to stage the event of the death. His first had been found in the park on a bench with no eyes, ears or tongue. A Sign was placed around her neck saying 'I see no evil, I hear no evil, I speak no evil, I am evil.'

The police were unsure whether the killer was talking about himself or the victim. The second victim cleared this up. The second involved two girls. Both had been cleaners in an office block at night and had the keys to the facility. They went missing one night and never returned to work, until Craig returned them a fortnight later. Craig had entered the office block for the second time with the girls and then killed both on site.

He took his time and staged the office to reflect the passage from the New Testament.

Zephaniah 1:2-6 "I will sweep away everything in your land, I will sweep away both people and animals alike. Even the birds in the air and the fish in the sea will die. I will reduce the wicked heaps of rubble along with the rest of humanity"

It was written on the wall above where the bodies of the two cleaners lay... Also with a cat, two birds and a bag of fish... Craig had emptied all the rubbish bins from the offices around them. Underneath the passage he had wrote were the words *I am evil, I am god.*

He had escalated from knowing what he was to who he thought he should be. Alex knew this was only going to get worse.

The fourth body was discovered three days ago. A young woman had been taken from shop on a Sunday a few weeks before. She was nineteen and unmarried.

The security camera in the shop had given the police the closest to a description of Craig they had so far. Against his M.O. he had been going in to buy supplies when the girl behind the counter seemed too laugh at the man in front of him. He was an elderly balding man. When he left Craig and the young girl had been the only two people left in the shop. He reached over dragged her from the counter and knocked her unconscious, she was just then carried out of the shop. Nobody around to witness other than the poor CCTV which was in the corner of the shop. Craig was a large man, wearing a baseball cap so they didn't really get a good look at his face.

The body had been found two weeks later in a church ... nailed to a cross with several quotes written on the floor underneath her.

2 Kings 2:23:24 NAB , Exodus 31:12-15 Deuteronomy 22:20-21 NAB These had all been found in the bible and basically summed up that she shouldn't have been working on a Sunday, sleeping with men before she was married and to top it off had laughed at a bald man... all points in the bible were punishable by death. Craig had not only read the bible he had swallowed it whole and was starting to act vengeance by it. Underneath the quotes it had simply read.

I am god, man's approval is not requested, required or relevant.

He wasn't going to stop here. Craig was on a mission. So was Alex, today though she needed to do right by her family first.

On arrival outside the house she asked Oliver to go and find Craig. He had been living in the same farm that his parents had left him. It was by all accounts his base of operations for the kidnapping.

Alex told Oliver to find him and follow him. That is all, don't approach him. She would contact him when she needed picking up. Either tonight or tomorrow morning. Alex got out of the car and headed up the drive. She knew this wasn't going to be an easy sell and it was going to take time. Her father and brother were going to be a problem. They were never easy to lie too. And that was what she was going to have to do.

Alex walked into the front door and through to the kitchen where her mum was washing up.

"Hi Mum."

Her mother turned and dropped the plate. She ran over to Alex and hugged her. Checking her all over as if she had just been in a car crash.

"Alex my Alex," She was holding Alex so tight the breath was nearly coming out of her.

Alex's father and brother had heard the plate drop from the porch and turned to laugh at her mother. On seeing Alex they both also ran into the kitchen.

Chapter Six

For some time they stood in the kitchen in a huddle as if to be discussing the next play against the Dallas Cowboys. In earnest they were just making sure that Alex was okay. There were a few tears in all their eyes.

"Okay enough now, give her some breathing space. Let's all sit at the table, I think you have some explaining to do Alex."

Alex had been working on her story in her head for the last three months. She needed to be able to explain her disappearance without explaining everything she had been doing. Her family loved her but they were also cops. They had a duty, much as she had before all this started.

"First I am sorry, sorry I haven't been in touch for a couple of months. I didn't know any of this was going to happen. When the captain suspended me after the Deacon James case, I was a little lost. All the stuff that had happened in the bar and Sophie. And when I arrived home there was an invite from who I presumed had been Maria Mellor to visit with her in Italy. I just thought the break would do me good."

"Maria is Michael Mellor's Sister?" Jason hadn't been as up to speed as his parents on the events before his sister's disappearance.

"Yes I presumed a thank you for saving her brother's life in the club. I packed a bag and decided why not. I was going to send you a postcard when I got there to surprise you all. When I got there it was actually Michael who had arranged it all. He was a nutcase and had planned, I think, to kill me. He said he was going to kill the people around me starting with Michael Simpson, Paul's brother."

"Why with him, I wouldn't have thought he knew him Alex?" She was afraid of this question as it didn't put her in a good light. The last time she had seen her parents she was showing off her new boyfriend Chris Masters. She didn't want to tell them that two weeks later she had cheated on him with Michael Simpson in a hotel the night of the funeral.

"I think he saw us at the funeral together, we had dinner later that evening and I think he has been following me."

"Did he kill Sophie?" Alex knew that question was going to be next. It wasn't a far leap to put the two together.

"I don't know but I would say it was a possibility, He attacked me and stole my gun, tried to attack me again in my hotel if it weren't for them I wouldn't have got away. But then I didn't think I needed to stop him, so I called his parents. Michael had taken a plane to England. I was scared he was going to go through with it, so Maria helped me get a plane to England to stop him before he did something stupid. I couldn't find him. Or Michael or his parents. I had another call from Maria, Michael had called her from Germany so I followed him there also to no prevail."

"When did you know the police were looking for you Alex." Her dad was looking her straight in the eye. She knew what it felt like to be one of his arrests now.

"In the hotel in Germany. I was sitting thinking what to do next and watching the TV next thing I knew I was on it. Freaked me out I swear. Especially knowing what he had done to Michael and Paul's parents. I got straight back on the plane and went to the police station and told them everything. They told me Michael was still missing and what had happened to his mum and dad. I couldn't believe it."

Alex started to well up in her eyes. Some was the relief to finally be spinning this story to her parents and some was the thought of Michael still in that cabin with his throat slit.

"Why didn't you come back home then?"

This was going to be a harder lie to spin. She knew her dad and brother would have put a watch on her passport so she needed to say to them she had been back for months. She needed an excuse to what she had been up to and she needed to explain the packages.

"I did, but I got involved in something."

"Something to do with Germany?" Alex hadn't expected that question from her father.

"Yes something to do with Germany. How did you know?"

"Alex up until about three months ago you had made one trip out of this country to the UK. During these three months you have been to Germany twice, Italy and again to the UK. It doesn't take a police captain to work out something is up."

"I was going to tell you. It all started with the Jack Quaid case. Remember I told you about him, the bloke that had all the boxes and killed himself. He was looking into something in Germany. And I am doing the same."

"What is it?" It took her brother to ask the direct question. She didn't want them involved. She didn't want them to be at risk should this whole thing collapse around her. She especially didn't want Christopher Mellor knowing that they knew everything.

"I can't say."

"Alex!" It was her father's strict voice. She had heard it before but mainly directed at her brother when he had done something stupid.

"Dad, I can't. I am working with some people and we are sworn to secrecy until we find out how deep this thing goes." She was using her police training here. She knew that there were cases that you weren't allowed to talk about. Her father had used those words on her and her brother numerous times. He would always tell them everything once it was public knowledge but not before.

"Tell me you are safe Alex," Her mother had been so worried about her.

"I am mum, I really am. Even have my own body guard. He is currently finding a hotel room."

"Does your Captain know you are working on something else?"

"I don't know. I was just told it was above his paygrade." Another good cop term to say that the lower ranks don't need to know. Alex was now believing she was going to get away with this.

"I am sure he will know soon. It's why I sent you both the packages. They were my copies so that when it comes time to explain all this it will become quite clear. You didn't open them did you?"

Alex's dad and brother both looked at each other.

"What packages?" Alex hadn't expected that.

"The packages I sent you when I got back into the country a couple of months ago. I specifically told you on the note not to open them?"

There was still a blank look on both of their faces.

"Alex we haven't seen any packages. That's why we have been so worried we haven't heard from you for three months. Dad knew you were back in the country which had been some comfort for mum. But that was all we knew."

Alex knew they weren't kidding.

"But I sent them. I even ensured that the guy in the delivery office put enough on them to get here."

"Well we haven't seen them."

Alex was worried now. Where had they gone? Losing one in the post was almost acceptable nowadays but not two. It took a while to sink in and then her focus was back in the room.

Her parents and brother standing staring back at her. She needed to continue the story. Her first thought was to log on and check her cloud accounts. But she needed them not to see her worry.

"Oh that's strange. I will print them out again so that you have copies."

Her father wasn't really buying any of this. He wasn't going to push it with her mother in the room but he needed answers on what Alex was up too.

"Have you been eating Alex; you look like you have lost weight. Doesn't she mum?" Jason had clearly been having the same thoughts as his father, He wanted alone time with Alex also.

"Make her some food love. I could go for a sandwich also." Alex's mother was already up and at the stove. They beckoned Alex to the porch.

"Come and have a beer with your old man."

Alex knew what was coming but she felt after ignoring them for three months she owed them something. She could at least show that she meant everything she had been saying.

"Your mother might be buying all this Alex, but we know you. If you are in trouble and trying to send evidence home to us then you are worried about something." They were almost on top of her as she left the house.

"I am not dad, I just don't want all this covered up. I can't tell you what it is but I will tell you that yesterday it involved the secretary of state, that's all I can say. It's that high up you just never know what will happen." That was the truest statement she had told since entering the house. Yesterday was all about the secretary of state.

"Alex just tell me you are not mixed up in this Avenger nonsense?"

Alex was looking directly at her father.

"The film?"

"No you know what I mean?"

"No Dad, I really don't?"

"Someone, or some people are killing killers Alex. They are calling them the Real Life Avengers. There have been dozens of cases lately where they are finding these bodies with either taped confessions or records showing what they had done."

Alex knew what he was talking about now. But she kept a straight face.

"I haven't heard anything?"

"The police are trying to keep it all under wraps as much as possible aren't they Dad. If you ask me at least they are killing the bad guys for us."

Alex's dad turned his focus to his son.

"Killing is killing. Nobody has the right to become judge and juror to these people no matter what they have done. They should face the court of law."

Neither of them answered their dad's statement. Alex knew how loyal he was to the force and his job. She knew he would not understand what she had been doing.

"When will it be over Alex?" Another question Alex didn't really want to hear tonight but she knew it had been coming.

"I don't know. It's not as simple as closing a case, there are other factors involved. Just know that I am safe and I will be back at some point. I miss you guys, the station the day to day job all of it."

"What do you want us to say to your team and your captain as they call nearly every day to see if we have heard from you?"

"Just tell them that I am safe and that I will be back."

"Arnie style then," Alex laughed at Jason. The laugh had been the first for a long time.

"Yes, Arnie style."

"Food's ready," Alex's mum called them in from the porch. They sat at the table and dropped the conversation around Alex and her work. Her mother was asking about Italy did she get to see any of it. She explained about the churches and the colosseum. The rest of the night was all relevant chit chat about how they had all been, what they had all been up to. Alex was staying the night. It was a long drive back to her apartment and whilst Oliver was out looking for Craig, a night's rest in her old bed sounded a perfect end for the day.

Morning came and she had slept in. Her father had already left for work by the time she went downstairs.

"Morning, Mum."

"Morning, sweetheart. Your dad came in to say goodbye but he didn't want to wake you." Alex's mum was at the sink washing the breakfast plates.

"I thought I felt him kissing my forehead but then thought it must have been a dream."

"I will tell him, he will like that, some breakfast?"

"No thanks I need to run an errand. But I will come back for a sandwich at lunch if that is okay?"

"Sounds lovely dear."

"Good, can I borrow your car as well mum? I didn't drive myself here?"

"Yes of course, you know where the keys are." Alex went and took them from the back of the door. She went over and kissed her mother on the cheek.

"See you in a bit." Alex was out the front door and straight on her phone.

"Hi," Oliver picked up straight away, as he always did.

"Hi, did you find him?"

"Yes, he is where we knew him to be."

"Is he alone?"

"Personally yes, I didn't see anyone else in the main house. I think he has the girls in the barn."

"Okay, let's deal with him tonight. I am at my parents and staying for lunch come and collect me about three."

"Okay. No problem."

Alex put the phone down and got into her mother's car.

By the time she had returned home her brother and father had come home for lunch also. They had come home to spend more time with Alex but also to tell her about the case they had just solved. They had arrested Martin Bates for the home murders. That was one off of Alex's to do list. Martin had been caught on camera trying to rob a house last night and one of the officers in the station recognised him. By the time they had called him in he already confessed to the double murder. It had been a good day at the office for them. Although he never knew it, confessing was the best thing Martin could have done, as Alex wouldn't have been in a forgiving mood. Lunch was over quickly, it seemed so anyway, it was like old times. Alex had to go. Oliver was waiting in the car outside. She gave hugs and kisses and promised to be in touch more and even make dinner on occasion.

Alex climbed into the back of the car. She could see her parents and her brother in the window as she left but resisted the urge to wave back at them.

Oliver moved off and drove for about five minutes before speaking.

"Good visit?" Alex hadn't expected a question. They had a very straight relationship and that was almost a personal question.

"Yes, thanks." Alex kept it brief in line with their previous conversations. Today, Oliver was in a chattier mood.

"Must have been nice to see them after such a long time."

"It was."

"Bet they missed you." Alex realised he wasn't giving up.

"Yes it had been too long. Won't leave it as long next time. What about you Oliver, do you have any family?" Alex thought she would take the opportunity to investigate. Oliver didn't respond straight away so Alex pushed some more.

"I don't think we have ever had this conversation?"

"No, Alex, no family, I was an orphan child. Think that's why I joined the army straight from school." That did explain his impeccable timing and dress sense. Always dressed in a suit and a tie as if it were a uniform.

"I am sorry to hear that."

"Don't be, it's been a good life and then coming out of the Army getting my commercial pilots licence and working for the Mellor's has been a good job." Alex believed him. He sounded genuinely happy.

"Do you miss the flying Oliver?"

"Not as much as you would think. I have always had a passion for it. But this break is doing me good."

"Jack of all trades aren't you, how about the IT, where did that come about?" Oliver was talking but still not looking backwards. He could see Alex leaning forward in the mirror to show she was interested in what he had to say.

"The army I guess. As technology changed so did it, they started to look for more and more experts in this field. Before I knew it I was full time at a desk running programmes and simulations. I enjoyed it. I did miss the fighting side of it though."

"So is that why you left?"

"No not really, I had done my time and the offer was on the table from a private security firm. They were going to pay for me to get the commercial licence and give me a job as a pilot / I.T. / Bodyguard to Mr Mellor. Sounded too good to be true. And to be fair to their word it has been."

Alex sat back and paused a moment. She didn't want to put him in an awkward position for the next question.

"What do you think of Mr Mellor?"

Now it was Oliver's time to pause.

"As a boss. He is a good one. We are all paid well and I do mean well. As a Father he has done the best with what he has. Maria is a wonderful woman and so is Carly. Michael however, he was always a handful. We have known what he was but Mr Mellor ensured that nobody else did."

"And as a business man?" Oliver paused for the second time.

"Don't really think I am in the position to know. Yes, I have accompanied him to meetings and on the plane. But I tend to keep away from the conversation."

"Good answer."

"No sorry I didn't mean it like that. I meant whatever he discusses I've tried to not have an opinion about."

"Tried?"

Oliver was silent again for a while. He seemed desperate to open up to Alex. But as Alex had been protecting her family, sometimes too much knowledge is dangerous.

"Tried, I guess this last thing. What we are doing here. I feel it was inevitable no matter what they all said."

"All?"

"What they said, is what I meant"

Alex started to realise Oliver had given a little more than he expected too. He knew a lot more than he was giving up in their first real conversation. She was silent for a little longer.

"Can I ask?"

"We are here." Alex turned around and looked through the window. They had arrived at the farm where Craig was residing. She could see the house and the barn in which they believed he was holding at least four girls in there.

"Can I still ask my one question before we get on with resolving this?"

"Yes, Alex, you can ask me anything." There was something in the tone of his voice that made her believe that that was true.

"How many trips have you made to Germany and Paris in the last ten years?"

There was a pause for a little longer this time.

"hundreds"

That was enough for now. Alex could have kept this conversation going all night long. Oliver had been in his employment for some time and clearly a valued member of the team. He would know things that she now wanted to know. She needed to understand fully the type of man she was dealing with, and Oliver would be her way in.

Chapter Seven

Alex managed to put the conversation to one side. Having been the closest that they had come to real talking between them in two months, she was keen to keep the momentum going but not now. Now there were more pressing events at hand, a few hundred feet away there were at least four girls in danger and Alex needed to help them. They were parked right at the bottom of the drive and across the road. Far enough to know that nobody could see them or imagine they were looking at the farm.

"I think he was here alone last night, well I say alone, I am presuming the girls are in the barn as he took over trays of what I believe was food. He was over there for a good hour before returning to the main house. The lights went on, one by one as he moved room to room and there was no sign of another person."

"Did you get a good look at him? Big bloke? Small bloke? The video image can be quite deceptive?" Alex had all the documents on him and a copy of the one picture from the store. The picture was grainy and taken from height so really didn't show depth very well. Her first thought was that people that work on farms are generally fit. She didn't want to get into a fist fight with anyone. Oliver handed over his phone.

He had taken a picture of Craig heading back to the house. It wasn't great but it did show him walking passed his truck.

"He is not a small lad, Alex."

He wasn't, he must have been six foot six inches tall. And about the same wide. It was no wonder none of these women had escaped from him.

"No he is not, jesus that is a big guy."

"Do you need any help Alex?" Alex was taken back by the question. Something had seriously changed in Oliver. Almost overnight he has become chatty and supportive. He was always supportive but not personally, only on a professional level. Later she wondered if it had been the fact that he didn't protect her against Christopher. The fact that Christopher had gotten to her and hurt her and he hadn't been there. There was almost a warming nature to him now.

"No, thanks for the offer but this is my quest and you don't need to get messed up in it."

"Alex, you may have already noticed, I am messed up in it."

"Not like me you're not." Alex didn't want to finish that sentence. She wanted to say you are not a hired killer, Oliver.

"It will be fine. I am not looking to wrestle the guy just…" She paused mid-sentence. She was going to say just kill him. But that sounded wrong.

"I am just going to get the girls out and deal with him." Alex knew what deal meant, and so did Oliver.

"I am going to take a walk around the premises see if I can spot anyone else."

"Be careful." Oliver once more sounded genuinely interested in her wellbeing.

"I will, thank you." Alex got out of the car and walked over towards the bushes.

Whatever was making Oliver like this was making her think about him, in more than just an employee, employer format. Today there was almost a human, caring, considerate side to him. There had been times over the past two months when she thought he was about to break into conversation but not like this. It was almost a shame to leave him.

Alex needed to put the new relationship with Oliver to one side, again, her mind was getting clouded with it, she had a job to do and that was to free these girls.

There was no alternative than to have to walk a long way out to avoid being seen. There were open fields on every side of the farm house and the barn. Anyone driving up would been seen a good five to ten minutes before arriving. Alex started on the long walk around the compound. Nothing moved the whole time she walked. She had a pair of binoculars to look at the barn and the house, but nothing, not a single movement. It took almost an hour to get back to the car where Oliver had been waiting.

"Anything?"

"Nothing, not a movement from the house or the barn. I am not even sure he is in there?"

"See the red truck, that's what he has been driving about in. He was yesterday and it was in the video from the shop. Well the top of it anyway. So my guess is that he is. Probably mid bible reading, or asleep, we know he likes to prowl at night. We are going to have to just go and see."

"Not before nightfall. He is going to see me coming a mile away in daylight. And a twelve bore shotgun travels a long way." Alex emphasised the 'me' in the context as Oliver had again said 'we'. She didn't want him to help her, she felt whilst he just did stake outs and IT work he wasn't as corrupt as she was. He wasn't police, there was some comfort in the fact that deep down Alex still believed she was police. This was police work. It just wasn't lawful police work.

"So, what do you want to do until then?"

Alex thought about it, she really wanted to continue the conversation she was having with Oliver earlier but felt it may distract her from the job at hand. Her head was already fuzzy with this new found openness.

"I suggest we try to get our heads down for a couple of hours. It may be a long night." Oliver wasn't expecting that answer but he didn't object.

Alex closed her eyes and laid in the back of the car. For the first hour she just laid there with her eyes closed. She didn't sleep, she was running over in her head the events with her parents, concerned that she hadn't left them with too much to worry about. Her mind then turned to Chris and James back in the office and the Captain. Should she go and see them whilst she is here or is that going to bring up too many questions, questions she really didn't want to answer. The more adaptations of the truth, the more chance that she was going to be found out. Alex had started to almost have a touch of sympathy for Chris. He had been into their relationship and had been falling for Alex. Alex could tell from the way his body language had changed around her since their trip to Germany. She had abandoned him with no call or anything. No, seeing them probably wasn't a good idea.

Eventually, Alex fell to sleep. The Mellor's had obviously been playing on her mind too, as that is what she had started to dream about. It was a beautiful day, Alex was on board a yaught with Maria, sun bathing on the deck whilst sipping cocktails. Both in their bikinis, as if they were beach wear models. Christopher and Carly were in the main cabin watching something on the TV and waving at the both of them. Maria had been telling Alex about a new guy she had met, someone she had a real connection with. It was Jack, Jack Quaid was the new guy and he was meeting them when they arrived in port. They were laughing and giggling about how cute he was and how lucky Maria had been to get to him first. Alex had her sights on him also but lost out to Maria, even in her dream she hadn't found a man, she thought about that sometime later when she was awake.

Maria had beckoned over to one of the waiters shouting for more drinks. She shouted that there was a chance of them sobering up at this rate. Alex could see all the waiters walking around, shirtless and looked like they had just finished a Chippendales concert. With black trousers, no shirt and a black dickie bow. They continued to laugh. Alex was laughing so hard it was hurting her stomach. One of the waiters came up and asked Alex a question.

"How many?" She hadn't heard him and continued to laugh with Maria.

"How Many?" Alex heard him this time, she turned at the question and prepared to say as many as you can carry, just keep them coming. As she did the boat disappeared and she had been in a darkened room.

"How many?" the man asking the question was now in the shadows. Alex was trying to get her bearings.

"How many?" He asked again and as he did he stood forward. It was Michael Mellor.

"How many, Alex?" Alex could feel her hands tied behind her back, she was no longer laying down on deck, but tied to a chair. Those steely blue eyes coming out of the shadows at her.

"How many, Alex?" The words just came coming. She struggled to get out of the chair but the ropes were cutting into her hands.

"Let me go." Alex screamed back at Michael

"How many, Alex?" The voice was getting louder and louder.

"Let me go, Michael."

"How many Alex!" Michael was shouting in her face now, he sounded so much like his father had when he had got angry. His face was so close she could almost smell his cologne. He stopped and stood back.

"No matter." the gun was placed to her forehead. Bang!

Alex jumped up from the back seat of the car, almost hitting her head on the roof as she did.

"Woo, woo, calm down Alex, think you just had a bad dream?" Oliver had hold of her shoulder to calm her down. It took Alex a while but she realised where she was.

"Yes, sorry, think I lost myself a little there. It's okay, I am okay, I will be fine." She moved Oliver's hand from her shoulder.

"Odd, I was listening to you murmur and it sounded a fun dream to be having at the beginning, I swear you were laughing in your sleep." Oliver smiled at her.

Alex remembered the dream. It had been so real, Michael Mellor, he really was the stuff nightmares are made of. The shadow, the eyes, it had all been so real.

"Was I? I don't remember." It was a lie but she didn't want to tell Oliver she was having nightmares about people she had killed.

"What time is it?"

"A little after eight thirty. The sun has gone down and it is as dark as it is going to get."

"Okay," Alex was waking herself up to bring herself back to the real world.

"There is a security light between the house and the barn so be careful not to trigger it as it's a sure fire way of getting attention. I think it is on the house as it activates when he comes out straight away."

"Thanks, I will, what about my…" Oliver interrupted her.

"Your bag is packed and in the boot, are you sure you don't need help Alex? He isn't a small guy. I don't mind, I would kind of enjoy it?"

"No I know, but I will be fine," Alex almost felt that their earlier conversation had been part of a dream also, but it wasn't, Oliver had really started to open up. She almost wanted him to be with her.

Alex got out of the car and stood in the fresh air. It was a sure fire way of waking herself up. She went to the boot of the car and pulled out her black bag. It had her gun, some rounds, some tools and Craig Curle's file in there, ready to be placed next to him when she had taken care of him.

She headed across the road and up the drive way. It was dark enough out there to not be worried about it. Lights had now appeared in the main house so someone was home.

Alex was about thirty foot from the main opening in the drive, when the front door burst open and the security light kicked in. She dived next to the fence but nobody had been interested in seeing her. Craig was carrying two large jugs and had a stack of clothing over one shoulder. He walked straight across the yard and into the barn. Alex stood back up, this had changed her plans. Her aim was to get into the house and deal with him and then release the girls. Now they were all together in the barn. She would have to revaluate once she got up to the barn, as she had no idea what she was going to find there.

Alex kept to the fence for the rest of the walk up to the barn. There was a fear of Craig bursting through the barn doors at any time. As she got closer she could hear a recording over and over again. It was someone narrating the bible. Sometimes in English and then again in Latin. Seemed to be coming from speakers inside the barn.

Craig had rigged this up and been playing this twenty-four seven to the girls inside in his hope to be able to save their souls. The main house had a version of this also, she could hear it in stereo. When Craig wasn't listening to the bible, he was reading it or preaching it. It had totally engulfed him.

Alex arrived at the barn door, it was slightly open and she could see into the barn. The barn had been set out as stables for horses at some point. Maybe a dozen each side of the barn. The stable gates had now been modified with the centre cut out of them so that you could see into them. The window part had been covered with wire mesh so there was no chance of escape. Alex counted at least a dozen girls inside the barn. There were only police reports for four other girls.

What Alex hadn't checked was girls from other states. Craig had been busy, he travelled up and down the country and captured anyone who seemed to be going against gods will. They were brought to the barn, prostitutes were a particular favourite. There were so many references to them in the bible, Craig had seemed fixated on them. He had considered them to be an easy pick as nobody really missed them if they didn't return for a week or two. Down and outs were another, whether they were on drugs or not, they were easy to pick up and discard. Craig was out to save all their souls, but if he couldn't he put them out of their misery. To date, he hadn't saved anyone's soul.

Peering through the crack in the door she could see Craig had the girls cleaning themselves. One by one they would come to the table where he sat, strip off naked and wash themselves in front of him. They would then disregard the night gown they were wearing and put on a fresh one. It reminded Alex of having to clean up before supper at home with her parents. As that is exactly what it was. The girls had obviously come accustomed to this as they didn't scream, fight or run. They all cleaned themselves for the hope of some food. She thought about running into the barn and taking care of business but there was quite a bit of distance between her and Craig. He had time to turn and fight back. She watched and waited for them all to finish. They had cleaned themselves and put on a fresh white nightgown and returned to their stables without saying a word. Craig picked up the dirty gowns and threw them over his shoulder, he picked up the two jugs and headed out of the Barn. Alex was around the corner when he came out. Again, she thought about attacking him but at the same time thought about those jugs in his hand being smashed across her head. She watched as he walked over and entered the main house.

Alex followed behind him. When he went in, she did a circuit of the house. She wanted to see if there was anyone else inside, she couldn't see anyone. She still wasn't convinced as she hadn't seen him today until now, so it was risky but she needed to go in. There wasn't anyone in the house, he was alone.

On her circuit she had seen Craig standing in the kitchen preparing what looked like a big pot of stew.

This was going to be her opportunity. She entered through the main door as Craig had done and walked through the hall way to the kitchen at the back of the house. Her gun was now in front of her as she pushed open the door to the kitchen. Craig had gone. The stew was still on the stove and the knife and vegetable peelings were next to it. She pushed the door a little harder and entered the kitchen.

Alex was unconscious for the second time in forty-eight hours. Craig had seen her walking around the house and stood to the back of the door when she entered. One swift punch from his gorilla shaped hands knocked her down and out.

"Alex." There was a pause.

"Alex."

Alex could feel her head being moved side to side and a throbbing at the back. When she opened her eyes Oliver was kneeling above her.

"Alex, are you alright?"

Alex was trying to get her bearings. Trying to keep her eyes open and focused.

"Oliver? What, what happened? Where are we?"

"I don't know, Alex, we are in the barn. He is back in the house."

"I was in the house wasn't I? And the next thing I know I am here and you are calling my name."

"Yes, I watched as you went in, but seconds later you were out again. Being carried by Craig across his shoulder. He brought you here, and I guess locked you in this stable." Alex could see the door open and the padlock now in pieces on the floor where Oliver had broken it.

"As soon as I saw him carrying you, I started up the drive way. I was across the road by the time he headed back to the house. Nearly met him heading back to the barn with some soup for the girls. I saw him place a bowl by your stable. I knew he hadn't killed you at that point. He left here about ten, fifteen minutes ago. It has taken me that long to bring you around." Alex was rubbing the back of her head.

"He certainly packs a punch. Either that or he hit me with a baseball bat. Where's my gun?" Alex was feeling around herself.

"I don't know? I haven't seen it. Craig must have it, it will be in the house?"

"Do you have a gun, Oliver?"

"No." Oliver sounded disappointed at that, as if he had been letting her down.

"I haven't been carrying it for some time, there wasn't a need. Never mind that are you ok?"

Alex was surprised he wasn't carrying a gun. She just presumed that all Christopher Mellor employees would be. She supposed at the moment though he was her employee. Christopher Mellor had handed him over.

"Yes I am okay. I need to get my gun back and end this," Alex tried getting to her feet. She was a bit wobbly but it didn't take long for the blood to rush back to her head and legs.

"What about the girls?"

"Still in their stables, I was more worried about you than them. I will say they aren't moving though Alex. I think whatever he gave them in that stew had some kind of sedative in it. I checked when I came past to get to you and they all seem to be sleeping. Must be powerful stuff to knock them out that quickly."

Alex took a moment to gather her thoughts.

"So, he is armed, and a giant of a man, and all we have on our side is a pitchfork and a dozen passed out girls?" They weren't actually the type of thoughts Alex liked.

"We, Alex, I guess that means you want my help?" Oliver threw Alex a smile and she in turn smiled back at him.

"We need a distraction, Alex. I will take the front door, you go around the back to see if you can get into the house and get your gun. I sense we are going to need it if we are going to take him down." Oliver kept highlighting the word we in all of his sentence. Alex did like the idea of having a partner in this. Especially after being knocked out. Another pair of hands was going to be useful.

"I agree, how are you going to distract him?"

"Leave that to me. I have an idea."

Alex and Oliver left the barn. They kept close to it at first as not to trigger the light. Oliver pointed to the back of the house and then without saying a word stepped into the light.

He walked straight up to the front door and knocked on it. Alex waited until she could see Craig heading to the front door through the side window and then headed to the back of the house.

Craig came to the front door of the house and opened the door.

"Excuse me sir, I saw your light on and me and my family have had a spot of car trouble. I was wondering if I could use your phone. Or maybe you could give us a lift into town? I am sure it's not far."

Nothing, no response. Oliver may as well have spoken to the door. It was smaller and only half the thickness. Craig just stood there looking directly at him.

"Sir, may I use your telephone? Or even a mobile if you have one?"

Still nothing, Craig just continued looking directly at him.

"Sir I am in a spot of bother, it will take two minutes just a quick call?"

Still nothing. There was a look in Craig's eyes that basically said 'move' else you will be tomorrow's breakfast.

"Sir, are you okay? Have you had some kind of speech problem? Is there someone else that I can talk too?" Oliver was looking behind him. Not to see if someone was in the house to see if Alex was in the house.

Still nothing. Craig's head started to move around as if to scope out if anyone else was watching. Oliver knew what was coming next. He could pick his stable in the barn if he wanted too.

"Sod it," Oliver threw the first punch which landed directly on Craig's chin. His head moved slightly backwards and then back to the same position. Then he just stood there. No response.

"Holy Crap."

Oliver's time in the army had taught him how to fight. In fact he had been almost invincible in training. When the first hit came, he knew this wasn't training. With the first hit, Oliver was off the porch and on the ground. He stood up as soon as he could with Craig slowly walking towards him. He was thankful he had knocked him so far as it gave him some time. Oliver rushed at him trying to tackle him to the ground. It didn't work. Craig was still coming forward and Oliver now had his arms around Craig's waist and was going backward. Craig hit Oliver square in the back and he was on the ground again. One kick from Craig had Oliver back on his back and looking up at him. With his left hand he picked Oliver off the ground, with his right hand he tried to knock his head back into it. Again, he lifted and punched, Oliver was losing consciousness at the second one he could feel his head start to glaze over. It was the sound of the gun shots that brought him back to reality. Alex had found her gun. It was sitting next to the sink where Craig had been washing up. When she came through the front door she could see Craig on top of Oliver pounding his head into the ground, she just aimed and put three shots into Craig.

He dropped Oliver, it almost looked on purpose. Not because he had just been shot three times. He turned and started to walk towards Alex. She fired again. Four more into his chest and one in his leg. He buckled slightly and straightened up and continued to walk towards her. She tried firing again but she was out.

"How many?" Alex heard the words coming out of her mouth as she had over a dozen times. Just has Michael Mellor had done in her dream not an hour ago. This time though it wasn't how many people have you killed? It was how many bullets is it going to take to put this man down. Her black bag was over by the barn she had left it there when she was looking at the girls bathing themselves. Alex ran along the porch and jumped off the end and ran towards the barn. Craig slowly turned and started to walk towards her. Still at the same pace. He didn't need to move fast for anyone. Alex opened the bag and reloaded. She then continued to walk towards him emptying the clip as she walked. The clip emptied in seconds and he was still standing. Not moving but standing in front of her. Alex later thought that it must have taken a lot of time for his body to register to his brain that it was dead. It had a long journey. Craig's knees buckled he was now kneeling in front of Alex. And with a thud he fell forward. Alex stepped back just in time. Or else, she would have been squashed under the fall.

She ran over to Oliver who was still lying on the ground.

"Oliver, Oliver are you okay?"

"Sorry I couldn't get up, I was trying, is my head still attached to my body?" Oliver's hands were up by his head.

"I know that feeling, yes your head, it's still all there."

"Good, because it doesn't seem that way, is he dealt with?"

"I hope so he took twenty something bullets to take him down. He just kept coming towards me."

"I am not surprised. The man was a tank, at least he punched like one."

Alex collapsed on the floor next to Oliver. They were both just lying there looking up at the night sky. Exhausted from the night's work, there was a sense of relief between them.

"I often wondered how these things went when I would be waiting outside for you. Are they all this intense?"

"No, not all. It's not often you have to take on Bigfoot," they both gave a little chuckle as much as their aching bones would allow.

"What do we do now?"

"Now, we take care of the girls. They probably need a medic and will all want to go home."

"They are all still drugged Alex, and there must be a dozen of them. We can't fit them all in the car."

Oliver was right. They weren't going to be easy to move. Alex stood up and walked over to her bag. Bringing it back and placing it on the floor next to Oliver. She took out Craig's file looked at it and placed it back into the bag.

"Maybe this isn't one for the real avengers."

"The what?"

"Nothing, just something my father was telling me. I have an idea."

Alex took her phone out of her pocket. And Dialled.

"My God, Alex?"

"James?"

"Alex where are you? You had us all freaked."

"I don't have a lot of time James, but all is good, I am good, I have seen my folks and I will be coming home soon. I will come and explain everything to you I promise." It sounded convincing but Alex knew it was a lie.

"I have just been driving past the old Curle Farm. You know past the rocket ship diner or whatever you call it. The one you like with the spicy nacho fries."

"Stars."

"That's the one. And there was a lot of gunfire coming from the place. At least twenty shots I heard. Can you check it out?"

"Okay, are you going to be there?"

"No, I have to go James, but please check it out as soon as possible as people maybe injured or worse. And James, don't tell the captain I rang you with it though. Just say you had a hunch or something. I don't want to be involved. I have enough on my plate as it is."

"Okay Alex, I will check it out. And Chris? Do you want me to say something to Chris he has been going mad looking for you? Every day he is searching for a sign or a word from you?"

Until this afternoon Alex hadn't given Chris a second thought. She didn't like the fact that he was still searching for her though. The guilt of the relationship ending was one thing. But for the guy to keep hope, that was another.

"No, not him either, this is between me and you James okay?" Alex paused. "No wait, tell him you heard from my parents and I am okay. And that I will be back soon. I promise."

Alex hung up the phone. Whatever Chris was or wasn't to her, he had been there to support her when she needed it. Whilst she was dealing with the confusion at the start of this mission of hers. It was Chris who had kept her feet on the ground.

"The police will be here in about twenty minutes. I just phoned my ex-partner." When Alex said those words it felt like they were wrong.

"When I say ex-partner, I mean ex police partner not partner partner." Alex had no idea why she was saying that to Oliver. She glossed over it and tried to move on.

"Let's open the doors to the barn and switch all the lights on so they can't miss anything. Then let's get out of here. Can you stand?"

"Yes I think so, see I am fine now," Oliver got to his feet and walked over to the barn with Alex. He was still a bit shaky but he didn't want Alex to see that.

"And thanks Alex, if it wasn't for you. I don't think my head would still be on my shoulders."

"Hey if it wasn't for you, I would be one of his captured girls washing myself at his pleasure."

Alex was spot on with the timing. James and two other squad cars were at the scene within twenty minutes. The girls were still drugged and passed out in the stables. They called for ambulances to revive them and take them to the station.

James hadn't told anyone of his conversation with Alex, and had said that he had a hunch about the guy after re watching the store video. The shooting was put down to an angry father rescuing his daughter or something like that. There was no telling how many girls had ever been kept in that barn. And with one busted padlock it was a plausible story. Whoever had busted the padlock at the end seemed to have left Craig Curle as a present to the police.

Alex and Oliver were long gone before they arrived. Heading back to New York, Oliver was driving and Alex was asleep within minutes of getting into the front of the car.

Chapter Eight

It took them, just under three hours to get back to the Waldorf Astoria. Oliver parked the car and lifted Alex out. He carried her through reception and to the suite. Unlocking the door, he laid her on the bed. After taking her shoes off, he fetched a warm damp cloth from the bathroom. Alex's face was covered in blood, splashing back from the bullets that were hitting Craig's chest.

Oliver gently started to wipe the blood from her face. As he did, Alex's hand lifted up to his as she opened her eyes.

"We're home?"

"We are."

Oliver continued wiping the warm towel across her brow and Alex let him. Alex closed her eyes, it felt good to be cared for someone who was actually there for her. Over the past three months her world had changed beyond recognition even to her.

She had slept with Chris out of necessity rather than love or passion. Some of it she believed was guilt. She had shared some of her theory with him and she was concerned at some point he was going to put two and two together. Especially about Sophie. Same with Michael, she had slept with him as he reminded her so much of Paul that day, Sophie's late husband. The man she had loved. And now, here she was lying on the bed with a man who was washing the blood from her face. He knew what she was and who she was. She raised her hand again still eyes closed and pulled him closer to her.

Kissing him on the lips long and lingering. She could tell from the kiss where this was going next, he pulled backwards and then slowly started to undress her, unbuttoning her shirt, undoing her trousers, Alex sat up and started to remove Oliver's clothes.

Not a word was spoken as they continued to undress each other until naked, standing they fell back onto the bed together. There was a slow lingering mood to the kissing, neither of them wanted this to be rushed and neither of them wanted to stop. Alex's hands were all over Oliver, he had kept himself in great shape since leaving the army she rubbed up and down his back and to his side. He winced with a hint of pain where Craig had kicked him. There was a pulling back from Oliver and they exchanged a smile with each other. Alex's hand became gentler. They explored each other for the first time, caressing each and every part of each other's bodies. Slowly as if not to miss anything. When Oliver entered Alex, the anticipation had been so great that Alex gave out a huge sigh. The love making was tender and purposeful, they had both at some point over the past months thought about this but never that it was going to be this intense, this heated. Alex had been having sex with Chris and Michael, just sex. This wasn't just sex this was the next level up, from what she had been doing. Alex lost herself into Oliver as he continued to enter her. With every stroke, touch, thrust she gave herself more to him. Time was lost to her, she was lost in the moment. As the night went on the pressure mounted and mounted until the pressure built up so much neither of them could control it anymore, and coming together they reached the climax.

Alex lay silent, her eyes had been closed but as she opened them Oliver was still laying directly on top of her looking at her straight in the eye. A smile came out of the corner of his mouth, Alex returned it.

He moved to the side of her, still holding her close he lay by her side. She snuggled into him. They didn't speak. They didn't need to, they both knew what had just happened. Within minutes they were both fast asleep. Alex's hand firmly in Oliver's. Both of them were lost to each other and the remainder of the night.

Alex sat bolt upright in bed. The sun was streaming through the window and Oliver wasn't there she was alone.

"Shit the files!" Alex's heart was in her mouth as those words came out. With the confusion and enjoyment of last night and the fight with Craig she hadn't reset the timing on the release of the files they would by now be winging there way to newspapers, TV stations the Brown Institute has gone viral.

She grabbed at the side draw and opened it, nothing was in there. She was sure her laptop should have been there. It was always there. She looked around the room, at the desk in the corner it was on there and open.

Alex hadn't remembered leaving it open when she left a couple of days ago. And where was Oliver, doubt started to creep into her mind. She jumped across the bed and to the desk. The computer was open and in the middle of the screen was a box with the words file deleted. Alex pressed esc. and it took her back to the main menu, she started to search her accounts. They were all there but they were all empty. All the information that she had uploaded was gone. Alex started to panic. Oliver had deleted everything, it was all a ruse.

It took her a while to notice but the background on the screen on the computer was one of a plane. Christopher Mellor's plane. Hers didn't have a background, her computer had just a black screen. This wasn't her computer it was the same make and model and it had all her accounts on it. It had her history, but it wasn't hers.

Alex looked up. Something was off and then she twigged, this wasn't even her room. Last night she had been asleep when Oliver carried her into his room. Alex headed back to the bed and got dressed her clothes were laid all over the floor. She needed to get back to her own room and check her own computer. She was just tying her shoes when Oliver came through the door. He was carrying coffee and tablets. Oliver had been to the pharmacy to get some pain killers as he was sure they were both going to need them.

"Morning, Alex."

Alex grabbed her gun from the floor and pointed it directly at him.

"What have you done?" Alex almost screamed at him which took him back, he placed the coffee on the side.

"Alex I can explain."

"Explain what? Explain that you have a clone of my computer in your room? Explain where all my files have gone? Have you deleted everything? Were they sent last night?" Oliver paused before he responded to her.

"No they weren't sent, Alex put the gun down. I was protecting you Alex."

"Protecting me or protecting your employer Christopher Mellor?"

"Protecting you Alex. I set a bug in your programme that if you didn't reset it would delete everything. You didn't really want to send those files out." Alex didn't, but she was too angry to answer him logically.

"Mr Mellor didn't want the files sending out, I did! When did you do this? When?" Alex's voice was raised and Oliver was trying to keep his low.

"About a month ago, Alex, what do you think Mr Mellor was going to do if any of this got leaked Alex. You would have been dead before it hit the news. You live a dangerous life Alex. And all I was doing was protecting you against yourself."

"You have had this running all this time. You have been watching me as I work on my computer. Spying on me for your boss," Alex wasn't listening to him. She couldn't decide what she was angrier about, the fact that she had found out he was spying on her or that she had let her defences down last night to him.

"And last night what was that all about to get closer to me, understand what's going on in my mind."

"Alex, no listen last night, you and I," Alex was nodding her head side to side.

"Alex you aren't listening?"

"Is my room bugged to? Is that how you knew when to answer the phone because you were spying on me. You could see me pick up the receiver."

Oliver didn't answer the question he just walked towards her.

"Don't, stay where you are," Alex's mind rushed back to the missing post. Her brother and father never received the information she sent them.

"Holy shit do you have the files also? The hard copies do you have them also?"

Oliver stood still not saying a word.

"Did you stop the post to my parents and my brother's house? Do you have the hard copies; Oliver just tell me?"

"It's protecting your family Alex. They don't need to be tied up in this."

"It's not protecting them. It's protecting him. What about the train station the airport, all of it all gone!! Is it all gone?"

Oliver didn't speak again.

"Out of my way."

"Alex."

"I said out of my way," Alex's gun was straight out in front of her and she meant what she said. Oliver moved to the other side of the room.

"Alex, just stay and listen to me. It can all be explained. Trust me."

It was too late, she was out of the room and running towards the stairs. Within minutes she was out of the hotel and heading to grand central station. The five blocks took no time at all. Heading to the reception desk and signed out her keys to the lockers. Opening one by one she found nothing. All the hard drives and the fingerprints were gone. Alex sat at the bench opposite the lockers. All her back up information was gone. There was no point running to the airports because if they already had these then she was sure they had them also.

Alex still had the original copy of the fingerprint in her purse. She didn't know why she had kept it but she was glad she had.

Twenty minutes of soul searching sitting on that bench, Alex walked back to the hotel. Her hard drive was gone but the tracking device was still there. She had kept it in the hotel safe and not in the room for fear of something like this happening, and now it had. Alex had been betrayed by the one man that she had trusted. It had taken her months to let him in and last night she had let him all the way in.

Alex needed time to think and this wasn't the place. Oliver had clearly still been working for Mr Mellor. She needed distance from him. Especially after the feelings that surfaced last night. She packed a bag, collected the tracking device and headed out of the Waldorf Astoria. She had expected Oliver to be waiting for her on her return but he wasn't. Her mind had him running directly to Christopher Mellor.

Alex wasn't going to get very far on foot, so need transportation. She hailed a cab and asked him to take her to the nearest car dealership. Which he did. Alex bought a new five seater black SUV. The card that

Christopher Mellor had given her was still working, Alex presumed Oliver hadn't got to the Mellor's yet. Either that or Christopher Mellor hadn't had time to cancel it. Alex still had everything confused in her head over the last twelve hours. She had used the card a couple of days ago, but it seemed like they have had the information for months, well at least access to her computer and the files sent to her parents. Why were they still letting her carry on if they thought she had nothing to blackmail them with? Why not just get rid of her?

After the purchase, Alex drove south for about two hours, originally she thought she was heading home for help from her brother and father, but she couldn't do that. What Oliver had said in the room was still ringing in her ears. He had been protecting her and her family. She would need to do the same. Alex couldn't help thinking that as far as Christopher Mellor was concerned, she was now just a liability, Christopher would be thinking she had no hold over him now so she was fair game to take out. What she didn't understand was why he hadn't done it already.

She didn't want her family getting involved in anything that may happen now. No, Alex needed to get this situation resolved and get back on with the job. Work was so important to her, it was who she was now. Alex pulled over in the next diner on the route. She had missed dinner last night and breakfast this morning and after the energetic evening she had with Oliver, she was hungry.

When the waitress arrived she ordered the works and sat in the window so she could see anyone approaching. Alex took a local paper from the counter. Partly to read and partly to hide behind. Home was about an hour from her, and you never knew who ventured this far out.

On the front page were the faces of two girls been missing for over a week now. These were both safe now, she knew that. She had seen them both washing themselves last night in the barn. James will have had them back to their parents by now.

Alex carried on through the paper whilst eating her breakfast. One story peaked her interest. About an hour drive west of where she was, a little town called Christiana. Two victims had reported to the police of being drugged and raped against their will. What had peaked her interest was that they were both male, claiming that a young blonde woman had done this.

The second man had claimed he feared for his life. She was stronger than she had looked and by the way she held her hands around his neck it had made him believe he was about to die.

Alex decided to check it out. She finished her breakfast and left the diner. Sitting in the car she booted up the tracking device, she typed in the place and time of the alleged attacks. Sure enough there was a Brown Institute child in the room. It was a woman called Andrea Stapleton. M&P. Murdering Psychopathic, these were rare in women from the institute but something had made this girl special. Alex no longer had the files so she knew nothing more about her.

It was going to be enough of a distraction for Alex to put the events of the morning behind her. She was also desperately trying to put the events of last night in the hotel behind her too but they kept coming back in her mind. Oliver's taste was still on her lips. His scent was still in her hair. Alex had hoped the food would help with that. It hadn't.

A case would help though, throwing herself into work was something she was good at. It was something she needed. Alex drove, as she did, the news on the radio stated that a man had been found murdered in his bed at home. In Christiana. Strangled. They were suspecting the same woman who had recently attacked two men.

Alex knew it was Andrea, the second victim had been correct, she was escalating. This gave Alex a purpose. The job had almost come as a release to her. She was more focused when she was on a case. When she arrived in the town she checked into a Christiana Hotel using her own card. She needed to limit the use of the Mellor card for the case of emergencies she was sure that he would be having it tracked by now.

According to the tracking device Andrea was in an office building in town. Perhaps working there. She headed over to the building to check it out. It was an estate agent's office.

Andrea was the manager of the business. Her families business. Her father had bought and sold real estate on a large scale. They were very wealthy international property tycoons. As a side business, Andrea's father had set Andrea up with her own little Business. Something local to where they lived, to keep her close.

Alex decided to go in. There was an attractive dark haired girl sitting at the first desk as she walked in. Two other girls in the office who were on phones, she could see Andrea in her office in the back of the room.

"Hi can I help you?"

"I don't know, I was driving through your little town, and loved the look of it. I was wondering if there were any houses for sale in the area."

"I am sure we can find you something, please take a seat, Mrs?"

"No it's Miss, Miss Mellor."

"Okay Miss Mellor. Now what type of property are you looking for? An apartment? A two up two down? The town is of average size but we cover the next couple of towns over also."

"I was hoping for something a bit larger than that."

"Okay, I have a nice three bedroom house here in the centre of town. It is walking distance from everything?"

"Sorry when I said a little bigger? I would say somewhere in the region of three to four million. I am looking to move out of New York and live a bit more, you know, rural?"

The girl was taken back a bit. Alex didn't look like she had that type of money. In fact she looked like what she was, the daughter of a cop who had been hit on the head a couple of times in the last few days. Alex hoped that the raise in money would get Andrea's attention.

"Bear with me a moment," the young girl got up and went through to Andrea's office. Alex could see them talking between and then Andrea followed the girl back to her desk. Her plan had worked. As Andrea got closer, she had all the features of a Brown Institute baby, she was stunning and could have passed for a supermodel. Alex knew it had not been hard for her to get men to take her home, they must have been lining up around the block.

"Can we help you madam?" Andrea's voice was to match it was soft and silky. This woman was really the real article.

"Yes, it's Miss, Miss Mellor. I was just explaining to this young lady here that I was looking for a house."

"Yes she explained, three to four million dollars wasn't it?"

"Yes that's right, are you able to help or is there somewhere else I should go?" Alex could sense from the tone of Andrea's voice that she didn't believe a word she was saying. So Alex pulled the black card out of her bag and placed it on the table. Andrea knew what it was straight away. She had been asking her father for one since she was fourteen. Although her Father was wealthy he knew he needed to teach Andrea the value of money. It's why he set the business up and made her work for a living.

"Thank you, Susan, I will take it from here. Would you like to follow me to my office it is more private in there?"

Alex followed Andrea back to the office and Andrea closed the door behind them.

"A Black card then, I have been after one of those myself."

"My step father gave it to me he is big in the oil world."

Andrea sat behind her desk and pointed to the chair opposite her for Alex to sit down.

"Please take a seat, can I get you a coffee or tea?"

"I am fine thank you." Andrea's tone in her voice had certainly changed since she saw the card.

"Ok let's see what we can find for you."

Andrea logged onto the computer. Instead of putting in a search for a property she Googled the word Mellor and Oil. Sure enough the search came up stating billions of dollars. Christopher Mellor's profile was in front of her. Alex credentials had checked out.

Andrea logged on to the main server for a selection of houses. She searched through them and talked Alex through three or four properties. Most on the outskirts of town as no property in town was worth that much money. Alex explained to Andrea that none were exactly what she had been hoping or looking for. So Alex had decided that she was going to stay in town for a few days to look around and hopefully they would meet again tomorrow with some more options on the table.

It had been tempting just to get it over and done with there and then. She knew what Andrea was, and she had been so calm about it, considering she had killed a man last night. On departing, Alex had dropped a subtle hint that she wanted to know what the nightlife was like. Both Andrea and Susan jumped at the chance with an offer to show her. They recommended a hotel, the one Alex had already booked into, and arranged to pick her up at the hotel at seven and take her for a few drinks. A night out with a billionaire's daughter was about the most exciting thing that could happen in the town.

Alex spent the rest of the afternoon in her room. She would have normally spent the afternoon looking at files but that had been taken away from her. At six she started to get ready. She still had the clothes that she wore in the park the other night, she figured these would be good enough to go out in in this little town. She wasn't going to be able to compete with the other two on looks but she needed to present herself to be in their company.

Alex's plan was going to be to stick close to Andrea and follow her home tonight. She could deal with her then, but Alex knew Andrea would still be on a high from the kill last night. This was a dangerous time she clearly had no remorse for her actions, attending work today like nothing had happened. Alex's fear was, with that little empathy, she would just continue on this path night after night. It was up to Alex to stop her now.

Seven p.m. came and Andrea and Susan were waiting in reception as promised. They looked pretty much as Alex had expected. Stunning. She was certainly the ugly sister of the three of them. Which Alex didn't mind as the last thing she needed tonight, was the attention of the male kind.

"Hi, I hope you don't mind but we have a gift for you."

From behind Susan's back she produced three cowboy hats.

"It is line dancing night down at TJs we thought that would be a giggle. Well that and it really is about the only decent bar in the town."

"Way to sell it Susan."

Alex laughed.

"Sounds great but I have to warn you, I can't dance."

"Neither can we, but the guys are cute and girls drink for free on dance night, so its win win."

"Now you say that, drinking, now that I can do."

Alex followed them out of the hotel. The bar was in walking distance. Most places in the town were. The bar was heaving when they arrived, there were tables all around the edge of the bar leaving a big space in the middle for dancing. And there were lots of people dancing.

To get to the drinks they needed to walk through the dancers. Susan was pulled off by a tall dark haired cowboy and started dancing immediately, Andrea and Alex made it to the bar without being mauled. Andrea ordered three beers and three shots as chasers.

"I love girls drink free nights," Andrea smiled at Alex. Then she gestured over to the tables. They managed to grab the last one.

"Wow its busy in here, is it always like this?"

"Busy yes, dancing not every night, but we town folk do know how to through a shindig. Normally twice a week, more in the holidays."

Susan managed to escape the dancing and was back at the table.

"Harder to get across than normal." she held up the bottle and gestured at the other two, they all clinked them together.

"To wild men with tongues of silver." Alex looked at Andrea at the toast that Susan had made.

"It's a thing, we make a toast before every new drink. Silly really but its tradition."

"Come on give it ago," Susan passed the shots to each of them.

"Okay." Alex was lost for a second, girls nights out weren't something that she was used too. Since leaving school she couldn't remember going to one. Most of her drinking habits had been with her father and brother or other people on the force. Police officers tended to stick together when drinking and didn't really socialise outside of their circle.

"To silver men with wild tongues," Alex laughed as she said it. So did the other two. The toasts came thick and fast over the next couple of hours. So did the attention from all the men in the bar. Andrea stood out a mile from the crowd.

Alex couldn't understand that given two of her victims survived an attack why she hadn't been singled out as the attacker. She was hardly lurking in the shadows. And there was definitely no mistaking her for someone else. The truth had been that she had been identified. She had even been questioned and at every occasion her father and a dozen witness's had an alibi for her.

Her father's property portfolio almost covered the whole town. Inclusive of the police station and the houses of most of the officers on the force. There wasn't a man or woman who was going to stand up to him, let alone arrest his daughter. Every man in the bar at some point had checked Andrea out or at least tried to talk to her. A few who had tried and failed even approached Alex as a consolation prize. Even if Alex had been minded to be second best she knew to stay on focus with Andrea.

One man in particular had been very focused on Andrea. In any other circumstances she probably wouldn't have looked at him. He was a nice enough guy, but there were hotter and more charming men in the bar. This worried Alex, Andrea was playing up to him. Alex presumed this to be the fact that he was a little smaller than the rest and could be easily over powered. Andrea wasn't looking for a mate, more of a victim.

The dancing stopped and so did the music, now all you could hear was faint tunes coming from the bar and people starting to leave. Alex could see Andrea coming back from the toilet. She had whispered something in this guy's ear and he past her a piece of paper. Something was going to happen tonight. Alex was right, she was still on a high, which was dangerous.

"Come on, we can walk you home."

"Thanks Susan, but it is not necessary I know my way."

"It's fine let us walk you, we want to, don't we Andrea?" Andrea was back at the table.

"Of course, we need to ensure nothing happens to our premier client."

They all laughed. Exiting together, the girls walked Alex back to the hotel. They made their goodbyes and promised to meet tomorrow in the offices to help Alex look for more houses.

Alex stood in reception and gave it a few minutes for them to go their separate ways. They did, Alex figured that Andrea had other things to do tonight. So she wasn't going to be hanging out with Susan.

Staying in the shadows, Alex followed Andrea across town. She had stayed quite a way back although it hadn't mattered. Andrea didn't turn once to look behind her. Andrea wasn't worried about being followed.

As she turned a corner she walked up to the door of a small and modest house and rang the bell. The guy from the bar opened the door. The joy on his face was unmistakable. He must have felt like he won the lottery. Not only did he pull the most attractive girl in the bar but he made her come to him.

He almost pounced on her on the door step. Andrea manoeuvred him back into the house. Alex didn't rush to follow her in, she presumed she was going to give him at least the satisfaction of a good time before killing him. She was wrong. By the time she reached the back door of the house, Andrea was already elbow deep with a knife in this guy's chest. Alex wasted no more time and kicked the back door in.

"Freeze!" As the words came out of her mouth she almost felt like a police officer again.

Andrea looked up from what she was doing. She could make out the gun but not the person behind it. She laid the knife down to the side of her and then she stood up, no panic or rush. Just slowly and purposefully.

"I said freeze, didn't I?" Andrea then recognised the voice.

"Alex Mellor, is that you?"

"Yes Andrea, it is me. I followed you from the hotel. What was up, didn't you want to give this one a good time? The last three victims at least got to have sex with you."

"I don't get it? You're the police?"

"Yes." Alex didn't like to lie about that. She wasn't sure herself if she was still police. The work she had been doing was police work, but the conclusions were hardly by the book.

"We have been watching you, sit down."

Andrea did as she was told. Her demeanour showed Alex that she wasn't upset with what she had done. There were no tears in fact there was no emotion at all. It was as if it was natural to her. Andrea never knew, but it was.

"Jesus Andrea, you must have attacked him as soon as the door was closed."

"I hadn't intended too, he was all hands." Alex half expected a *he came at me. I was defending myself. What else could I do?* But she wasn't going to get that from Andrea. Andrea knew what she had been doing. She didn't look like she particularly enjoyed it though which was strange. The blank expression on her face was worrying to Alex. It was cold.

"Good enough excuse I suppose, especially to have at him with what now looks like a potato peeler?"

"What can I say, some people just have to die Alex." With that Andrea sprung across the table. The rage took Alex by surprise, her face changed in an instant to someone that wanted to hurt Alex. The gun was knocked from her hand.

Before she knew it Andrea was on top of her punching at her shoulder and side of her head. Alex managed to turn her over but the kicking and punching didn't stop. Alex was fighting back as they rolled around on the floor. The second victim had been correct, she was stronger than she looked. Alex could see the gun on the floor near the back door but she wasn't going to be able to reach it. Not with Andrea between her at the door. Alex had taken a couple of blows to the head recently Andreas punches didn't really seem to be affecting her. They continued rolling around on the floor. It was real cat like fighting pulling hair and biting. Alex kept getting the smell of fresh blood from the body next to them it was either that or the blood that was pouring out of her nose.

Andrea had manoeuvred herself to the back door and made a jump for the gun. She tried to kick back at Alex as she was on the floor as leverage. Alex grabbed at the potato peeler and plunged it into Andrea's calf dragging the peeler towards her. The pain stopped Andrea from crawling forward towards the gun. She turned and grabbed her calf. Alex pulled it out and lunged forward and stuck the peeler straight into the side of Andrea's neck. The blood spurted everywhere. It was over, Andrea wasn't getting up from this. Alex lay almost on top of her exhausted, looking directly at her.

She hadn't realised but for all the time it took for the life to bleed out of Andrea she had kept hold of the potato peeler in her throat. Time just seemed to have stopped.

It was a few minutes before Alex snapped out of it and started to think. No file to leave, nobody was going to put the two and two together unless she told them. She was going to have to find a way of doing this. Alex stood up. She was covered in blood again. There was no way she could not walk across town like this.

Alex took off her shirt and washed herself in the sink. She tried soaking the shirt but the blood from the two dead bodies behind her was never going to come out. After washing herself she then walked the dead guy's house. She found a fresh T shirt upstairs that fit her, due to the guy Andrea had choose being close to her size. She then returned to the kitchen took the gun and the potato peeler and placed them in a bag with her shirt. It was ruined but her thought process had been that she didn't want to leave evidence. Other than her blood which was hopefully mixed up with everyone else's. Leaving by the back door, within a minute Alex was back on the street. Taking her time with the walk back to the hotel. She reflected on what a difference a day had made. Yesterday she had a partner who helped her with all of this. For the first time he had become a real partner. In work and in life. She spent the night in Oliver's arms, and tonight she was going to shower, sleep and then work on a plan to sort her situation with Christopher Mellor.

Alex wasn't paying attention as she entered into the car park of the hotel. If she had been she would have noticed the black van was a new addition to the car park, as she passed it the side door slid open, and three men got out, they took her with ease. She felt a small prick into her neck and then the night went black.

Chapter Nine

When Alex came around she was still in darkness. There was a hood placed over her head. As she breathed she could taste the cloth. Her hands were tied behind her back. All she could think of was the dream she had had the night before. The dream of Michael Mellor standing over her with a gun. She knew that wasn't going to happen, as Michael was dead. She had taken care of him months ago.

Alex tried to check herself out, other than feeling a bit groggy from the injection, she seemed in one piece. Other than being hooded and her hands and feet were bound together and to the chair she was okay. This stunk of Christopher Mellor.

"I know you are there, and there is no need for this I am not scared. Take this hood off. Christopher." There was no response to Alex's shout out.

"Christopher Mellor, I know this is you I know this is your handy work. Look we have things to discuss. You aren't as clever as you think."

Still nothing.

Alex continued to shout for another ten minutes with no response. She then heard someone entering the room. There was some muffled talking and then the hood was whipped off of her head. The bright lights hurt her eyes for a little until they were acclimatised. Alex was sat at a long boardroom like table. There were closed shutters all around her and in front of her were four men. All dressed in black suits with white shirts and black ties. Each of them had ear pieces in. She recognised three of them from the abduction and presumed the fourth would have been driving the van.

"Where am I? I want to speak to Mr Mellor."

Nobody answered. They were all looking directly at her, but nobody responded to her plea.

"I said where am I? And untie me. This is nonsense we can sort it all out."

Still no answer. There was a message come through on one of the ear pieces. The man closest to the door opened the door.

Through the door came a familiar face. Not the one she had been expecting though. Alex sat face to face across the table to Victoria Owens. President of the United States, Victoria Owens. Alex could hardly breathe at the shock of who had just walked through the door.

"Do you know who I am, Miss Keaton?"

"Yes Mam." Alex's voice was soft and low. This must be it, they knew what she had been doing. The president of the United States knew her name. What was confusing Alex at that moment was she barely warranted that? A visit from the president.

"Good, then at least one of us is in the picture, can you tell me who you are Miss Keaton?"

"Alex Keaton, mam?"

"I know your name Miss Keaton, but who are you and what is your involvement with Mr Mellor?"

One of the guards leant over and whispered into the president's ear.

"Whom I am informed, you thought kidnapped you and brought you here. Which I must say has me even more intrigued now?"

Alex was confused. If they didn't know who she was? Did they know what she had been doing? And what would have brought the president of the United States here? How much did she know already? Was she here for Alex or here for Christopher Mellor? Alex was thinking fast on what to say.

"Let us start with something simple, do you work for Mr Mellor Miss Keaton?" Alex paused that wasn't a simple answer.

"I wouldn't say that I worked for him, no Madam President."

"Do you work with him then Miss Keaton?"

"No I wouldn't say that either. He is someone I know, Madam President," Alex was trying to say as little as possible.

"Someone who you would believe to kidnap you and do you harm?" Alex thought about that but not for long.

"Yes Madam President, I believe he would if he had the chance."

The president sat staring at Alex. There was something very unnerving about sitting across the table to the most powerful woman on the planet.

"Then we may have more in common than I first thought Miss Keaton, can I call you Alex?" Alex nodded in response. The expression on the president's face had changed to a more relaxed one. This was helping Alex's nerves.

"I need some answers to some very serious questions and I need you to be straight with me. Are we clear Alex?"

"Yes Madam President"

"Good, I will tell you what I know. I know that you attacked Stephen Henderson in Central Park. I know it was probably self-defence as I also know that he had attacked two girls and killed one." Alex was a little shocked at this. Her first thought was that the president knew nothing. She was going to argue at that point but from the way the president spoke. When she said she knew. She really knew.

"All of which is currently being covered up by my Secretary of State and Mr Christopher Mellor." There was almost a relief from Alex at that statement. She had watched as Victoria Owens climbed the political ladder and was a big supporter of everything she had done. The first woman president and the first real voice of the people. It had been a landslide victory. Nearly every woman in the country voted for her including Alex.

"What surprised me was that Mr Mellor's men then attacked you and took you to the Waldorf Astoria. At this point you became a person of interest to me. We followed you to your parents' house and then again to the Curle Farm where you engaged in an attack on a Mr Craig Curle who has recently been indicted with six counts of murder and nineteen counts of kidnapping. Obviously you killed him, so he is not going to be facing charges. All in all, I think you did us a favour by dealing with it. Even if by unorthodox methods." Alex heard the words dealing with it. That is what she had been doing for the last three months dealing with the problem. It made her trust the president a little more.

"Following that, you returned to the Waldorf Astoria and that is where we lost you. That is until you checked into a hotel using your credit card."

Alex had been using her credit card so as not to let Mr Mellor know where she was. She didn't know other people were looking for her also.

"As you can see Miss Keaton I have questions. Why would Mr Mellor attack a victim and take her to a hotel? What is your involvement with him and how did you know about Mr Curle and the twelve girls in the barn?"

Alex was thinking fast. Was it time to come clean on all the events? She knew she wanted to trust her. If she did she was going to need immunity from prosecution. Were they even going to consider it? Especially if she confessed everything she had done? Alex had dealt with a lot of people not just Mr Curle. What were there interests in Christopher Mellor? It didn't sound like they were on his side? More looking into him? Is this the way to get to him? Alex was thinking as fast as she could, but it came back to the same point she didn't trust anyone in knowing what she was doing. No matter how high up the food chain they are. She was going to need more information before she parted with her story.

"I don't work for Mr Mellor, Madam President. I had some trouble with his son a few months ago. It caused me some distress to the point that I have taken time out of my job to take a holiday."

"And your involvement with Stephen Henderson?"

"He attacked me in the park, as you said. He then confessed to the murder and the attack on the two women. I didn't want to get involved, I had been away from police work for the past three months and wasn't ready to start again. I decided the best option was to leave him with his confession and leave him in the park." The story fit so far on what the president had been briefed on. Her secret service had been ordered to follow Stephen outside his own detail and this was all in her report.

"Why would he confess to you Miss Keaton? Hardly something one does to a total stranger?" It was a good point. Alex had slipped up with saying that.

"I don't know, I was a little over powering and he may have had the impression that I was going to hurt him." The president looked again hard at Alex, she was hardly menacing. Five feet four inches and as skinny as a rake.

"After the confession you wrote something on his chest and left didn't you? But then you went back, why?"

"I wrote his confession on his chest and took a photo. I thought someone else can deal with him. I went back because I thought about making a call on his phone so someone found him sooner. I didn't like the thought of him being in the park all alone. No matter what he had tried to do to me."

"And then, Miss Keaton?" The president was back to using her full name. That made her think that she wasn't trusting what Alex was saying.

"Then I presume I was knocked out by one of Mr Mellor's men. I woke up about six to seven hours later in my hotel room."

"Why do you think that is? Did you know he had been following you?"

Now she could come up with some truths and see how much that the president knew.

"Mr Mellor was waiting for me when I came around. I was asked if I was still investigating his son and him. I wasn't, I was then asked about my interest in Stephen Henderson. I didn't even know his name but Mr Mellor was very concerned about that. He proceeded to tell me that his family, the clinic in Germany and Stephen Henderson were all off limits. I was not to get involved in anything to do with them. He was deadly serious on that point. I must admit he was that serious, it peaked my interest."

"The clinic in Germany?"

"The Brown Institute in Germany. Something that Mr Mellor had some interest in. After the first altercation with his son in the nightclub. Mr Mellor wanted to thank me for saving his life. He knew that my partner and I had been struggling to have a baby and as way of a thankyou he sent us there for some tests. I am not sure why he brought that place up as I hadn't given it a second thought. Shortly after my partner and I broke up so we didn't get the results or anything." Most of what Alex was saying was true and if they checked records everything would stack up. She had become really good at spinning these stories to fit her situation. Especially when under pressure to do so.

The president hadn't flinched at the mention of the Brown Institute which led Alex to believe she knew nothing of it.

"Then what happened, Miss Keaton?"

"Then he let me go, well I say let me go, he left. I promised him I wasn't up to anything I was just taking a break."

The president wasn't buying anything that Alex was saying. The look on her face told Alex that.

"Miss Keaton, in all the time I have known Christopher Mellor, the one thing I can say for sure is that he never just drops it. He is far too stubborn for that." Alex knew her story was weak but she had to persevere with it. She shrugged her shoulders and continued with her story.

"My friend and I then took a trip to my parent's house. Over dinner my father and brother were talking about the case of the missing girls I didn't say anything to them but I always disliked Craig Curle I had known him from the town. When they showed me the picture from the video tape in the store. I thought that had a good chance of being him. I wanted to check it out for myself. I guess the talk of the police work got me thinking about returning to work. I discovered the girls in the barn and somehow got mixed up in it all. My friend and I were both attacked by Mr Curle but we managed to get the better of him." Alex was trying to keep eye contact all the way through the conversation but it was hard to do with Victoria.

"The better of him. I understand twenty shots were recovered from Mr Curle's body? Why didn't you report it to the police and stay around for the reward and recognition?"

"Again, after everything that had happened. Mr Curle, Mr Mellor, the events up state with Deacon James. I wasn't ready for the lime light again. I am not sure I am now. I just wanted to be left alone. So I telephoned it in anonymously to my old police station." The president lent backwards in her chair.

"That was you too was it Miss Keaton? Deacon James? I read about it and that a woman detective somehow stumbled across the bar of the most notorious serial killer of our time and apprehended him. I say apprehended, I mean killed him and his colleagues in the bar." Alex knew what she was saying. Another serial killer which you have dealt with Miss Keaton. Alex needed to be careful as she was leading the president to look closer at her.

"Yes Madam President. It has been a hell of a three months" Alex didn't respond to the point she was really making.

"Tell me about the events of last night Miss Keaton." The president changed the conversation.

"We just went back to the hotel in New York."

"No, last night Miss Keaton." Alex tried looking through the blinds. She could just about make out daylight. She had no idea how long she had been out for.

"Last night when we picked you up outside the hotel, you were carrying a gun a bloody knife, well what I gather was a potato peeler, and a blood stained shirt? Do you have an explanation for this?"

Alex was increasingly noticing that this story was becoming less and less viable by the moment. Coincidence was one thing, but murderer after murderer was hard to sell. Even with her knew found skill.

"The gun was for my protection from Mr Mellor." Close to the truth and to show that they were seemingly on the same side.

"The knife and the blood stained shirt. That was a different story Madam President"

"That's okay Miss Keaton I have all the time in the world to listen to your stories." Alex wasn't going to get out of this she was sure. She couldn't just lie to the president of the United States about how many murderers she kept just bumping in to.

"I was staying in the hotel. I had decided to take a road trip to clear my mind before perhaps returning to work. I met Andrea and Susan in a bar. We all joined in the line dancing and they were kind enough to lend me a hat so that I could fit in. They walked me back to my hotel and I realised after about five minutes, that I still had Andrea's hat. I wanted to return it. She had met a man at the bar and told me she was going back to his house. It was walking distance. I decided to drop it off now as I wanted an early start. I nearly caught her before she went in. When I got to the front door I could hear screaming. I went around the back and found her stabbing the man on the kitchen floor. We fought and eventually I got the better of her."

"So she is in custody Miss Keaton?" It was a loaded question from the President.

"No Madam President. During the attack the knife, potato peeler cut a vital organ and unfortunately she didn't make it."

"So we only have your word that she attacked the young man Miss Keaton?" Alex hadn't thought about it that way. The president was right. It was her fingerprints on the murder weapon that she still had. She could have killed them both. Alex had lost focus. Before she was meticulous with the files and the evidence and here she was being interrogated by the president with bloody clothes and the murder weapon in her possession.

"That is how it happened Madam President. I assure you. The last thing I am is a murderer. I was on my way back to the hotel to report it to the police. I believe Andrea had been the woman they were looking for. There were two attacks and one murder in the past three weeks. Two murders now."

The president was silent. One of her men leaned in and spoke in her ear. Basically saying that most of what she was saying had credibility. Although Alex was clearly lying about something.

"I will tell you what I think Miss Keaton. I think that death is certainly following you. Is it coincidence that your life seems to have developed around murder and violence? You are keeping things from us Miss Keaton, which you will answer at some point." The president then stopped. Alex almost predicted the next word. There was something more to this than just Alex.

"But for now I need your assistance. Although Miss Keaton, be assured we will be discussing this in more detail in the future. For now though, I want to talk to you one to one." The President nodded at her staff and they all left the room.

She walked down the table and sat next to Alex.

"Woman to woman Miss Keaton. How ever you are mixed up in this your actions in the last three months that I know of…" The president paused again at this point. A sign that she knew there was more to come.

"Your actions have shown that whatever you are doing? Or you are trying to do? It is for the right reasons. The way you are going about it is wrong. And we will discuss that at a later date. This is good news to me Miss Keaton. Because I need someone on my side."

"Alex," Alex wanted to be friends with the president.

"Alex, I am going to level with you. There is something rotten in the Whitehouse and my government. I believe it all has something to do with Mr Mellor. He is one of our biggest campaign sponsors and in return he had favourable contracts on our oil an electronics. That is just how it works in politics. Or so I thought. But now, now I am not so sure. His name keeps cropping up in policy debates and European and African Contracts. I swear that I wake up some mornings and wonder who is actually running this country, him or me."

Alex feared Christopher Mellor's reach. She never imagined it went all the way to the president of the United States and that she was worried about him. Christopher Mellor just became even more dangerous than Alex had thought.

"I need to know more about what Mr Mellor is up to Alex. I need someone to get closer to him. Discover his agenda and then help me clean up the government. This is my first year in office and I never believed in my wildest dreams how bad it had got. Can you help me Alex?" She looked genuine to Alex.

"Madam President, what can I do?"

"You have direct contact to Mr Mellor don't you? Is there a sense of trust there?" Alex wasn't sure there was trust, he had been going behind her back and collecting all her evidence. What Alex didn't understand? For some reason he was allowing her to carry on with her quest at his expense. He actively wanted her out there working on these cases.

"I guess there is Madam President."

"Then I need as much information as possible on him. I need to know what he is up to and how close he is with my government. His movements, his projects. What is this Brown Institute in Germany? Why is he so worried about you looking in to it? In general, why is he so worried about you? You must mean something to him. He obviously values you or fears you. I am unsure of which?"

"Madam President," Alex stopped as she said it. She wanted to say madam president I am unsure how effective I am going to be. She also wanted to tell her everything. There was something about her that screamed trust me. They were alone and up close and personal.

"Madam President. I will do everything that I can for you."

Alex Paused.

"Things have happened recently. Things I will need help with." That is all she said.

"I am sure they have Miss Keaton. But that is in the past and lets both leave it there for now. Now we need to trust each other." The way she said that almost made Alex believe she knew. Did she know that Alex was the Real Avengers? That is what her father had called them. They both exchanged a nod.

"What we need now is everything to return to order. Mr Mellor can't know that we have met. I need to know what has been going on and how many of my staff are involved. Get close to him Alex and get me any details or evidence that you can. Alex, if you need anything, one of my colleagues will give you a direct phone line to the Whitehouse and we will give you all the support we can. I need more information before looking to deal with Mr Mellor. I have tried but there are few I trust now. So I can't put my own people on this." There was something about the way that the President said deal with Mr Mellor. It almost felt as she wanted to dish out the same justice as Alex had been doing.

"Okay Madam President. I will do everything I can… Am I free to go?"

"Yes Alex you are." The president got up and tapped on the window.

"Madam President, where are we?"

"We are about thirty minutes north of the hotel you were picked up at last night. One of my men will take you back to the hotel" The four men re-entered the room and Alex was untied. The president nodded at one of the men and they handed over a mobile phone to her.

"If you need anything, call, and I will do everything I can. I will look forward to speaking to you soon Miss Keaton."

"Yes Madam President."

Alex was handed back her bag with the gun, potato peeler and the blood soaked shirt. True to her word, Alex was back in the hotel thirty minutes later.

She was now a tool for Mr Mellor and against Mr Mellor. She checked into her hotel room and lay on the bed. She had no idea what to do next. All she needed was some time to think. She looked at the clock on the wall, it had been almost midday. Whatever they injected her with must have knocked her out for a good ten hours. All of this drugging and clubbing to the head made Alex tired though. She drifted off to sleep as she lay on the bed. It was three p.m. when she woke.

Alex hadn't eaten since breakfast in the diner yesterday and with the drink consumed last night she had a hunger for some carbohydrates. She ordered two club sandwiches and a bottle of coke from room service.

When it arrived she took out her phone, a dozen missed calls and forty-three messages all but one from Oliver. Asking her to ring him. He just wanted to explain. She deleted them all without reading the rest them. There was another message from James saying thank you for the tip off yesterday and hoped she was okay. She wasn't. She was alone in a hotel room. She had blackmailed and killed the son of one of the most powerful men in the world. Lied to the president of the United States and to date killed at least two dozen people in three months. Things were far from okay and she needed a plan.

Chapter Ten

Alex devoured her lunch. There was still the smell of blood in her hair so she jumped into the shower with the hope of it waking her up and refreshing her mind. It didn't help. Her next steps weren't clear. Whilst her purpose was still to work her way through the task ahead of her. She now had the added thoughts that Christopher Mellor and the United States president maybe watching, waiting for her to do something. Whatever came next it was going to be challenging.

Andrea had been a welcome distraction from the events but now she was going to have to do something else. She packed up her bag. Her only thought was to keep moving and make sure that when she was, she wasn't going to be followed. With the tracker and her night bag in hand she went to leave the hotel room.

"Hello Alex," as Alex opened the door to leave and Oliver was standing in the door way. She dropped both bags but before she could grab her gun. Oliver did.

"Not this time Alex." Her next instinct was to punch out at him she threw one punch Oliver blocked it. As he did he stepped forward into the room. He wasn't alone. There were three of Christopher Mellor's goons standing behind him in the hall way.

"Now, now Alex we aren't here to hurt you."

Alex walked backwards into the room. Her gun was gone and there were four strapping ex forces guys standing in front of her. There was no way out.

"What do you want Oliver?"

"Sit down and we will explain."

"I want to stand."

"Alex just sit down. If we wanted to hurt you, we would have stormed the room whilst you were eating your club sandwich or when you were having a shower."

Alex sat on the edge of the bed.

"What do you want?"

"Mr Mellor just wants a conversation Alex. He just wants to talk to you about what has happened. Nothing has changed Alex. You just didn't give me time to explain."

"Shit nothing has changed, you have been working behind my back at collecting all my evidence." Alex was standing again now.

"Alex." Oliver could tell by the look in her eye she wasn't going to let this drop. She was hurting, she felt betrayed by him especially from the events in the Waldorf Astoria.

"Look we have been sent to collect you. I promise you we are not here to hurt you but you can either just jump in the car with us or we can take you."

Alex was ready for a fight but she knew she wasn't going to win.

"I have a car."

"We know, give the keys to James and he will drive it behind us. You can have it back when we leave Mr Mellor's" Alex wanted to scream, 'There is no us leaving Mr Mellor's, I want nothing to do with you. You stole my files from my room and emptied my safe places. You have taken my security.' She knew it wouldn't do any good. She was going with them. She grabbed her bag and pulled her keys out of it.

"James!" one of the men stood forward.

Alex walked to him and handed the keys over. As she did she grabbed his shoulders and lifted her knee straight to his groin. He buckled and within seconds he was on the floor in pain. There was a rush towards her.

"Woo! I owed him that for knocking me out." Oliver jumped in between the team and Alex.

"Come on calm down, James take the car. Everyone else with me. That includes you Alex." James got up and gingerly walked ahead of them.

Alex knew it was useless to fight against them and being knocked out or drugged for a fourth time in as many days didn't seem appealing to her.

Alex sat in the back of a black SUV next to one of Mr Mellor's goons. Oliver sat in the front. He tried to strike up a conversation with Alex at least a dozen times on the journey to no avail. She wasn't rude but only gave one word answers. Oliver knew he was getting the cold shoulder.

To her surprise they drove directly to Mr Mellor's Mansion. She had expected a dark and dingy warehouse somewhere.

On Arrival, Mr Mellor and Maria Mellor were finishing up an early dinner.

"Alex, so good to see you. Are you hungry? Do you want to join us?"

Maria just smiled in her direction. She had liked Alex, but she wasn't exactly buying the story of her brother's death. Maria knew what her brother was, but today she was still missing him.

"No, I am good."

"Oh, okay if you can wait in the study we will be finished shortly."

Alex turned towards the study. She had been there a few times before and knew her way. Oliver and James both followed her in.

"Sit down Alex."

"I will stand, thank you." Oliver took the fact that it was four words and a thank you at the end as progress. He nodded towards James and he left.

"Just going to be awkward aren't you? Where did you go?" Alex didn't answer that time.

"Alex this is silly. The files, all the information, it was taken so as not to fall in the wrong hands. It was a month ago at least. I spoke with Mr Mellor it was for the best"

"I am sure you did, and the best for who Oliver?"

"Alex, all of us, what I did was protect you from investigation. If I hadn't, those files would have been public knowledge wouldn't they? Just because we slept in and you forgot to change the time and date." This was true.

Alex hadn't intended for the files to go public unless something happened to her. And all that had happened to her that evening was that she had sex, good sex.

If the files were public knowledge by now, they would have been traced back to her. She was convinced she would have been caught by now. Either that or Mr Mellor would have dealt with her.

She was about to reply when Mr Mellor and Maria walked into the study. Oliver stood back and placed himself between Alex and the door.

"Alex, what happened? Where did you go?" Christopher and Maria sat on the sofa and gestured for her to do the same. Hesitantly she did.

"You know what happened!"

Christopher looked up at Oliver.

"I know, you went to Oliver's room looking for him. Discovered the lap top and then disappeared?" Oliver hadn't told them about the night. It wasn't that he had been ashamed, far from it. He had been totally into it. He just was keeping it from his employer.

"You took the files and cloned my laptop."

Christopher looked at Maria. Then so did Alex, she was surprised to see her in the room. She had thought that he would have wanted to keep it from her. The Brown Institute was hardly going to be a hot topic of conversation for her.

"It was for your safety Alex, I told my father to do it. We have had the files for over a month. The laptop, yes, Oliver put a programme in there to delete the files should you not reset. We didn't want to spook you. And your copy of the file was taken after you left the hotel for the first time. We needed to know you weren't about to do something silly." Alex was shocked. Maria knew everything and was on board, when did this happen?

"My father has explained everything to me Alex. And I am so glad we have you to help clear all this up. What those people did to us is nothing short of monstrous."

"He has? He has explained everything?"

Maria looked directly at her father.

"Yes everything, he has explained how he didn't know any of it had happened. What they had done to us at the Brown Institute and how he then bought into the company to try and find a cure. My father has sunk millions into the centre in order to see if they could reverse what they had done."

Alex sat back a little, looking directly at Christopher Mellor. He was as skilled as Alex at taking a story and twisting it to suit the situation.

"You see Alex, nothing has changed. You don't need to hold a gun to my head for me to help you. What you are helping us to do, is nothing more than patriotic act for your country. You're a national hero Alex." There was the politician coming out. Alex couldn't help but think what are you trying to do to your country Mr Mellor? He too had a presidential sound about him. She hadn't noticed it before, but she could hear it in his voice now.

"You still have the card I gave you? The tracking device? The fingerprint. And Oliver has the hard drive taken from your room. Things are as they were Alex. We have a job to do, together. I want us to finish it Alex well as much as we can."

"And the Brown Institute?"

"It's in process Alex, just google Brown Institute Germany. You will see that there is a redundancy announcement on line and the closure is within the next ninety days." He looked genuine. Maria picked up her phone from the table in front of her and googled it. Passing it over to Alex. Sure enough there had been an announcement. The headline had said due to lack of funding.

"The board just signed off on that did they?"

Christopher Mellor looked a bit uncomfortable with that question. It was the way that Alex had said the board. As if she knew more than he thought she had. Alex was just testing him. She knew that recommendations had been made by the board. Which he must have been party to.

Christopher Mellor glossed over it.

"Yes they understood that the research hadn't brought any conclusive results in over twenty years it was time to put a stop to it. Michael is gone now. I had no need to keep living the pipe dream. Whatever he was Alex he was my son and I wasn't able to save him from what they had done to him."

Maria grabbed her father's hand. He was good, he would make a perfect politician. Maybe even president, Alex didn't know how high he had his sights.

"I am sorry to hear about Michael, Maria," now Alex was playing the game to see how much Maria really knew. They both looked directly at each other.

"Thank you, after Italy, father tells me you couldn't find him?"

"No, sorry I tried. I just seemed to always be a few steps behind him."

"And he killed that man and woman in England, your friend's parents? And then a father and daughter in Germany."

"So I understand Maria, again I think I was just to slow in catching him. When I saw on the news that I was a person of interest in the murder of the Simpsons I needed to go back and deal with it. I wished I had caught up to him first."

They didn't break eye contact. The room was silenced. Christopher knew what Alex was up to with the testing of Maria.

"So where do we go now Alex. Do you want to continue on this road together or have you finished and want to go back to the day job? It is your choice Alex? Either way we will make your life as comfortable as possible after everything you have tried to do for us."

Comfortable as possible. Those words stuck in Alex's head. She was sure he could she was sure that he could give her money and she could just retire. She wasn't sure she could live with herself, knowing that these people walked amongst them. There was a breed of murderers and psychopaths at every corner and she knew how to find them. It was her job to find them and deal with them. It felt like a calling to her.

"Alex, we have trawled the list, there is a lot already in prison or dead. Some yet to come of age. Which although my father can't find a cure, my mother and I have come up with a foundation and they will receive anonymous donations and scholarships, which include counselling and guidance where we will do all we can for them." Maria was genuine. She had taken her father's story hook line and sinker.

Alex thought for a moment. She didn't believe the story that Christopher had spun. Not with the recent intervention from the president of the United States. No he was up to more than that.

"What about my hard drive?"

Christopher nodded over to Oliver. He passed it too her.

"In the interest of full disclosure Alex I will say that Oliver has put a fail-safe on the hard drive. Nothing has been deleted or tampered with it has been in his possession all the time. We need to ensure this information doesn't get out in the public." Alex knew that that was aimed for her to try and trust him again.

"I will take it from that Alex you wish to continue on our current path?" Alex took a deep breath before replying.

"I think we still have work to do Mr Mellor."

"Okay that's good news Alex. Is there anything more that I can do for you? You have all the equipment. Money. Do you need anything else?"

"I want resources Mr Mellor. Can I take James?"

"James and Oliver it is Alex"

"No, just James."

Oliver stood forward. Christopher nodded at him and he stood back. Alex didn't trust him anymore. Not after what they had done together. Not after the night in the Waldorf Astoria.

"Okay, if that is what you want Alex."

Alex picked up the hard drive and headed out of the room. She didn't make eye contact with Oliver or the Mellor's. Christopher nodded at Oliver and he followed.

"Alex?"

She was already at the front door before Oliver caught up with her.

"Alex, let me come with you."

"No, James will be fine. I don't need any other distractions." Oliver knew exactly what she meant. Alex was heading out of the front door.

"Alex, this is dangerous. I don't like the thought of you alone. I want to be with you." Oliver had hold of her arm and she pulled away.

"Seems I am always alone Oliver. I just never knew it."

Alex got into her SUV the tracker was in there and the keys were in the ignition. James followed in his own SUV as she went up the drive and back into society. Oliver and Mr Mellor were on the porch watching as they go.

"What now sir?"

"You follow them. Keep far enough back and don't engage with them."

"How long for?"

"For as long as it takes for her to burn out Oliver. The board are nervous enough at the moment and this is at least keeping them sweet by knowing we are at least attempting to clear out some of the undesirables."

"Okay."

Mr Mellor went back into the house and Oliver walked over to another black SUV and followed up the drive. He had a good idea where Alex would go, there was only one place she felt safe at the moment.

Chapter Eleven

Alex decided to go back to the Waldorf Astoria. It had become her safe place over the last few months. It was a good three-hour drive so she had time to think on the way there. Truth be known, she would have much preferred Oliver to be close to her. She would have preferred he was the one following as they headed to New York. Even after the betrayal he still seemed genuine about caring for her. The night they had together was still fresh in her mind and she couldn't wipe it from her memory.

On arrival, she spoke to reception and got a spare key for James to have Oliver's suite. Once she threw her bag and tracker on the bed she noticed the clock. Another day was over, it was almost eleven p.m. The events of the day had Alex's mind racing all over the place. There was little chance she was going to be getting sleep anytime soon. She opened the bedside cabinet. Her laptop was still there. She loaded the hard drive. Using the search engine, she looked for all documents associated with the board. Twenty-three thousand found. This wasn't going to be a straight forward search. She knew that the Brown Institute policy had been to only accept recommendations. That is how she and Chris had obtained entrance on their first visit. But now she knew the board were making recommendations. Now she needed to know who the board were.

The next couple of hours was spent doing just that. It was clear that they were playing it safe. Every document that she opened was either password protected or it just had initials. There were board meetings on spend and staffing levels. Also further recommendations. If it was recommended in the board meeting the person or people in question were always referred to as patient x or y in the minutes. This wasn't normal behaviour. What they were hiding, was well hidden.

There didn't seem to be a way to decipher what had been going on. This is when she knew Oliver could have helped her. A few days ago she would have trusted him too. But now she was alone. James was next door but she knew he was a company man. No one else would knock a woman unconscious. It was of little matter, Oliver wasn't there.

Alex decided a few glasses of wine would probably be a better end to an otherwise awful day. She packed the laptop to one side and switched on the TV. As she did she headed to the fridge. It had been restocked. Grabbing two of the small bottles of wine and filling a large tumbler she lay on the bed. She flicked through the channels finding an old black and white movie. A little escapism was a fitting end to the day. Six little bottles of wine later Alex was asleep.

It was seven thirty a.m. when she awoke. The TV was still on and the movie had disappeared, it was now the news. Alex phoned room service and ordered breakfast. The past few days had seemed like a blur this morning, and she was returning to normal. When breakfast arrived she sat on the bed eating her omelette. On the news they were pulling a body, or parts of a body, at least one person, out of a lake in Michigan. Lake Margrethe neat the Huron National park. Alex turned up the volume.

"Early indications from local authorities is that there are at least three sets of human remains found in the lake. A couple of skinny dippers last night uncovered this when they took a moonlight dip and an arm floated to

the surface. This twinned with the three bodies found at various sections of the 72 in the Huron National Park over the last month has local people concerned that this in fact is the work of a serial killer."

Alex heard at least six bodies and the words serial killer. That was what Alex needed, to be back to work. Well she didn't need, it was more of a desire to get back to normality or whatever passed as normality nowadays.

Alex pulled out her laptop to check where the National Park was. It was at least five hours west. Through Flint and Detroit and the town of Grayling was slap bang in the middle of the lake and the forest.

Alex had been planning to work her way west at some point and what better time than now. If she checked out and got on the road it would put some time and distance between her and Mr Mellor also. Time that she could use to research the board some more. She rang Oliver's room for James but he didn't answer. Another reason to miss Oliver, she had known he would answer almost immediately. It was time to shower, pack and then head out of New York. Alex did just that, by the time she had showered and packed, James had returned to his room from breakfast. She loaded up her SUV and took the five-hour drive to Grayling.

Alex missed Oliver more as she drove, she knew she could have worked all the way there with Oliver driving. Alex didn't want to share a car with James. Alone gave her a feeling of a bit of freedom from the Mellor's, sitting with a company man for the whole journey wouldn't have done that. Besides, she still didn't know James or his skills, besides knowing he could deliver a knockout blow. He was one of Mr Mellor's guards so there was a good chance he was ex-forces somewhere and he looked like he could handle himself.

Alex arrived at Grayling, driving through the town she looked for a hotel. Spicy Bobs, Spike's Kegger, Alex could tell she was in a classy place. She found a hotel at the north of the town, called The North Hotel. This was going to have to do. She hadn't passed anything else. Her plan was to check in and then start to do her research. Somewhere in this town was someone she wanted to meet.

The hotel room left a lot to be desired, she had been spoiled at the Waldorf Astoria to the life of luxury. She booked into the honeymoon suite in the hotel as it was the best and gave James the second best room. It was just a double room to be fair, there was only one premium room. On check in she picked up the local newspaper in reception, this gave her a place to start. There was nothing about the bodies in the lake but there was about the three previous killings. There were two bodies found just off the 72 and the third was also by a lake. They had all been there for some time so in various states of decomposition. The local police had put the murder down by ShellenBarge Lake as the first. This made Alex wonder whether the bodies recovered last night were also pre the two on the 72? Maybe this guy had a thing about the water. Whoever he was, they were estimating sometime in the last month. Alex just typed day by day into the tracker the location and then she did hour by hour. There was nothing. This wasn't what was expected. Was this person just a normal serial killer? Was there even such thing as a normal serial killer? She was convinced as a child she never heard of the amount of killings that she did today. Were there normal serial killers? Something Alex had forgotten existed.

On the plus side it was going to need some real police work to resolve. Alex was half excited about the fact that she couldn't just walk up and locate the killer straight away.

It didn't take her long to think again. The newspaper had said the bodies were found there. Didn't mean they were killed there, almost certainly the ones on the side of the road would have been thrown from a car or a truck. The bodies in the lake hadn't been killed on site if clearly if they had been chopped up first.

Alex started to think like a killer, she had spent so much time hunting them down thinking like them had almost become second nature. At first, whoever this was had spent time trying to cover their tracks, the cutting up of the bodies and driving the pieces to the lake, trying to weight them down to get rid of the evidence. That was all signs of guilt. That would have been at the start. As they enjoyed it more and more the guilt would have started to vanish. Maybe it was their plan with the fourth victim again by the lake. Deciding just to throw it in and save time. This lake was more deserted and off the beaten track, easier to get in and out of unseen. Maybe that's what the killer thought, but a passing person? Something may have spooked him. Now, whomever had been doing this hadn't even bothered to hide the bodies, they were almost rolled out of a car into the side of the road for anyone to find. The killer no longer had any guilt to worry about and just did what he did for pleasure. If it wasn't for the fact that there was little light on the road, surrounded by trees, they would have been found a lot sooner.

Alex widened her search. Grayling as a town and the surrounding areas hour by hour for the month. It took two hours, but eventually there was one Brown Institute baby in the town.

Paul Grayling, the great grandson of the founder of the town. This couldn't be a coincidence. Alex grabbed the hard drive and the laptop. Paul Grayling M&P&O the cocktail of any good serial killer.

He was at an address on the other side of town. Alex checked the time. The research and the drive, all of it had taken its toll. It was almost six p.m. She decided to take a drive to check it out but that was going to be all tonight. She thought about ringing James to come with her. But she didn't. If it had been Oliver she would have.

Through the town she could tell it wasn't an affluent area. The houses were run down and the people sitting outside them or walking the streets didn't look well to do. Well, that was until she turned up just off the 75, the main road going north on the town. There was a dozen or so houses that stood out a mile. They were to rival Christopher Mellor's. At the top of the drive was the address that Paul Grayling was still at. Alex had the tracker on the seat next to her in case he had moved on the drive over.

Grayling was spelt out on the gates. Alex hadn't been surprised he had come from money. It was fast coming apparent that they all had some kind of wealth. This was the Grayling's house, and this was their town.

Security was tight, she could see cameras and security guards in the grounds. This wasn't going to be an easy case for Alex to deal with. She sat a little bit back from the main gates and observed the grounds for a little while. Nothing and no one was coming in and out. The guard circled the house almost all the time. She was sure there were two on the outside. One by the main gate and the other circling. It seemed that someone was always watching.

It was time for James to earn his money. Alex went back to the hotel and spoke with him. She asked him to observe the place over night and then report back in the morning. James was certainly a soldier. He just nodded and disappeared in his SUV.

Alex figured if she was going to find out more about the Grayling's, Spikes Kegger was going to be as good a place to start as any.

Alex didn't bother to get changed. She washed her face in the sink and took the short drive down the road. Alex at her worst was still going to stand out in the town. She wasn't disappointed. The bar was relatively full but most people were sitting alone. This had definitely been a drinking bar. Alex took a seat at the bar.

"Can I get a beer please?"

"No problem, coming straight up."

The bar tender wandered over and placed a Budweiser in front of her.

"You're a new face?"

"Yes, just passing through."

"Passing through? To where exactly? This is hardly the centre of the universe." The bar tender threw a smile in her direction whilst glancing his eyes to look around the bar.

"Detroit."

"Oh that way, you don't sound Canadian."

"No I am not, was just visiting friends. Hi I'm Maria."

"Michael." The bar tender held out his hand. As he said his name, Alex had a flash back of Michael Mellor in her head and nearly didn't shake it. He didn't look like Michael, pushing sixty and didn't have all his own teeth.

"So what is there to do in this town, what was it called Greyly? Something like that?"

"Grayling. Maria this is just about it. Welcome to the busiest place in Grayling."

"Grayling, sorry, odd name? And really this is my highlight is it?"

"Named after the founders, they own pretty much the whole of it. And other places. Yes, ma'am we all pay our rent to the wonderful Grayling family. One way or another." There was a sound of defeat in the bar tenders voice.

"I sense from your tone they are not that wonderful?"

"Na, not that wonderful, half my customers in here are drinking as at some point they have been fired, screwed over or lost property to the Graylings."

"So they are good for your business then."

The barman looked back at her and smiled.

"Never really thought about it like that before. I guess they are. Although their rent keeps going up each month. Which doesn't really help me. Another?"

Alex hadn't realised but she had already finished the first beer.

"Yes, thank you."

As he walked down the bar he just filled three of the shot glasses that were sitting on the bar in front of guys who looked like the world was on their shoulders. He fetched another beer for Alex and one for himself and brought them back to her.

"So this is my option then is it, you are not just saying that to keep trade are you? If I go for a walk around the streets I am not going to find a nightclub a few trendy bars that sort of thing?"

"No, you're not, Spicy Bobs down the road has a bar but in Grayling it's just him and me. He generally looks after the food whilst I provide the real drinking in here. And I wouldn't suggest a walk around our streets at the moment." Finally, Alex had an opening to talk about the town.

"Why not?"

"Would seem we have a serial killer on the loose in these parts." Alex gave the customary look of shock.

"Really? Now that is a desperate ploy to keep me in here isn't it?"

"Somewhat ma'am, but it's true you not been listening to the news?"

"No sorry, my road trip has been pretty much me, Janet Jackson and a little motown. When? Who has been killed?"

"We aren't really sure. From the town it looks like we may have lost one of our own. Annabel Hamlyn. Cute girl, sorry woman. She had been missing six weeks or so. But people often go missing in Grayling to turn up again a few years later. From the local towns and all the way down to Flint there were at least a dozen missing people."

"A dozen? You're kidding me."

"Nope, three bodies found just up the road on the 72 and they have been dragging the lake for the last twenty-four hours. Jack down there reckons at least five so far."

Alex looked down the bar.

"Jack?" What was this place, she just needed a Christopher, Chris, James and Deacon. And you wrapped up her last three months in one bar.

"The old boy at the end of the bar."

Alex looked. That wasn't her Jack, this guy was eighty if he was a day. Almost looked like he was a down and out. Scruffy hair and hadn't shaved in a month.

"Five eh? How does he know?"

"He is the Sheriff around here."

That stopped that train of thought going through Alex's head. If she didn't get answers she was going to present herself to the station in the morning and offer her services. There was no point doing that now. Not if he was the man in charge.

"Jesus, not a lot of crime in these parts I hope?"

Michael laughed.

"No not a lot, this is the event of the decade. Probably the century. Jack just keeps order when it needs it. Generally, we all fall in line to the Graylings wishes anyway."

Alex pumped the barman for information for the next few hours. By the time she was back at the hotel she had chapter and verse on the Graylings.

Paul still lived at the main house with his parents, Cory and George. Paul was being groomed to take over the family businesses. Having just turned thirty it was his time. The Graylings owned everything. All the property in town was owned by them and rented back to the residents. Across the 75 there was an industrial estate that provided the food. The Graylings owned the rights for all the game on the national park. The fishing in the lakes and opened bakeries and ready meal plants. If you lived in it, ate it or worked in the town, you were owned by the Graylings.

The street where they lived was basically the handpicked foot soldiers. Managers of each of the businesses. They were kept close so that the Graylings didn't need to deal with the common man.

That wasn't going to make it easy for Alex to get close to him. From the info she had gleaned from the barman and he had in turn from the sheriff, her womanly ways weren't going to do it either. Paul was into blondes and not brunettes, she was convinced that Annabel may have been his trigger as the sheriff had a photo of her. She was stunning. Without seeing Paul she knew what the Brown Institute babies looked like. She knew there was going to be an attraction in there somewhere.

Since then, the three bodies that were found were all male. Whatever had gone on it wasn't looking like a sexual killing. There was little else Alex could do tonight. She did put the tracker back on to see where Paul was and he hadn't moved. He was still at the house and she knew that James was outside. Should something happen whilst she was asleep she was convinced that James would call.

Alex was back in the honeymoon suite. She looked for a mini fridge. There wasn't one. She called down to reception and asked for a bottle of wine. She was given the directions back to Spikes Kegger. This wasn't the Waldorf Astoria, sleep was about the best thing she was going to do tonight.

Alex was woken by knocking on her door. She threw on the robe and grabbed her gun and put it into her pocket. She wasn't taking any chances given the last few days.

It was James.

"What time is it?"

"Just gone eight a.m." Alex had slept soundly through the night. A good eight hours, something that never normally happened. She put it down to all the whacks to the head she had taken lately catching up with her.

"Was it a quiet night?"

"No, not really. Although I will say, an unexpected one."

"Really? Let me throw some clothes on and we can have breakfast at Spicy Bobs. It's just down the road turn left out of the hotel. Give me five minutes." Alex closed the door and threw clothes on. James was already there in the restaurant before she arrived. They ordered and sat in a booth by the window.

"So, eventful you say?"

"Yes, eventful, not at first, I didn't see a movement all night, but after one a.m. it was. I almost missed him leaving."

"Paul Grayling?"

"Yes, Paul. I think I was falling asleep. It was the sound of the Ferrari leaving that woke me up." James was shaking his head as if to re-in act waking up.

"Ferrari? They really do have all the money in this town, where did he go?"

"It was about twenty minutes outside of town, Camp Grayling the army base."

"Really, army? Didn't pick up anything last night to say he was in the army?"

"He is not, but it would seem he has some special friends there?"

When James said the words special friends he held up both hands and made the speech mark gesture with his fingers.

"What kind of friends?"

"Special friends."

Their food arrived. They waited for the waitress to leave before carrying on with the conversation. The problem with small towns is that you never knew who you were next to. And this town certainly had an allegiance to the Graylings.

"Special friends as in?"

"Well I followed him to the base and he was waved straight in. I still have my credentials so I pulled up and showed them to the guard on duty, I just said that I was with Paul Grayling. He didn't question me and just lifted the barrier." Alex had known James was forces. It was the way he carried himself. All of Mr Mellor's men did.

"I followed him to what looked like a car hanger. He knocked on the door and walked straight in. I watched as others, men and women arrived one by one. Didn't seem to be many couples entering."

"Did you go in?"

"I did, wish I hadn't. I can't forget what was going on in there." James had a shocked look on his face.

"What was in there?"

"I think every kind of sexual deviant there is, was going on in there. Men with men with other men, girls, and whips chains, there were men in gimp masks being whipped by girls in Heidi costumes. Honestly, and that was just in what I presume was the staging area."

"You are kidding me, really? A swinger's party?" Alex now had the same shocked look on her face.

"No, not just a swinger's party. That would have been tame by comparison. I wandered through all the bodies having sex with each other, and the men being treated like dogs and licking women's boots, to the back of the hanger. There they had made dry wall rooms. Four or five if I remember. There was all types of weird shit going on in there and you could just watch. Someone was making a movie? A woman was tied to like a swing then one by one men were coming in and, well, taking their turn. One man was being flogged with a proper whip and everything… and in one of the rooms what I think was water boarding. For fun."

"No shit."

"No shit, and I think your Mr Grayling is running the whole thing. He was certainly the main man and he ran the bar and paying the ladies if you know what I mean. Some were there by choice and I had the distinct impression that some were being paid to attend."

"The torture, and water boarding, you sure that's what it was, it was for real."

"Alex, this was not my first experience of waterboarding. And it was real. There was a queue to give it a go." Alex believed him when he said that.

"Then I think we may have found our murder scene? Things go too far and then they dump the bodies? What do you think?"

"Very possible. There were some really mixed up people in there Alex."

"Possible. Let's go back tonight. We can join the party."

Chapter Twelve

After breakfast they returned to the hotel. James to sleep and Alex to research somewhere to shop. If she was going to fit in, it sounded like she had to fit in as one of the call girls. She didn't have army credentials so it was her only option. There was nothing in Grayling with regards to ladies shops. She was going to have to take the drive to Flint. She did, shopping wasn't enjoyable for Alex. Today's shopping particularly, she spent the afternoon buying underwear and a long black trench coat to cover herself up with. Alex also bought a blonde wig. She had a hunch that it would attract Paul Grayling and plus she was the new girl in a very small town. She wanted to disguise herself as much as she could.

Alex was back in the hotel by mid-afternoon. She left a message with James under his door to meet tonight at nine p.m. They travelled together to the Grayling residence and sat at the end of the road. Far enough down so that the Graylings couldn't see the car. There was only one road in and out of the street so they could wait for him to leave at the bottom of it. The night was uneventful. Alex spent the night feeling uncomfortable with James. All that she was wearing was underwear and a coat. She had never worn that type of underwear for any man that she had been with and here she was sitting in a car next to him. The next few nights didn't get much better. Each night she sat there blonde wig on, in her basque stockings and suspenders covered in her long black cloak. The fourth night of sitting out in the car was the charm. Around eleven p.m. the Ferrari exited the drive. It headed across town followed closely behind by the SUV. The camp was twenty minutes away. Paul went straight in and they followed. The guard on security had questioned the couple coming through, Alex undid her coat. She was ushered straight in.

It was the same at the door to the car hanger. Alex's coat was undone and it was a done deal. James followed closely behind her.

James hadn't been exaggerating as they entered the hanger, there were sofas and bean bags everywhere, and each of them had people sprawled across in various stages of undress and sexual activity. Alex weighed up the room. There was a make shift bar in the corner, and where they entered almost felt like the staging area to the real event. The dry wall rooms at the back of the hanger were all in use. There were no doors on the room just as James had described. If you wanted to watch you could watch.

Alex was looking for Paul. He was stood at the bar. He had dressed to impress in a light blue suit with a white shirt and a blue tie. Alex needed to make her approach she fixed her coat so it was barely hanging from her shoulders. Everything she had was on display.

Alex went up to the bar and spoke with the barman.

"Can I get a beer please?"

"Sure."

Alex just stood with her back to the bar and watched the room, as some in the room were watching her. Including Paul. Up close he was a Browns baby, he had dark curly hair and blue eyes, sparkling blue eyes almost the same as Michaels had been. She kept catching a glance of him out of the corner of her eye.

"Excuse me, can I buy you a drink?"

"I am good thanks," Alex lifted her beer to show him.

"Let me buy you one anyway," Paul beckoned to the barman. He proceeded to start making a cocktail.

"Didn't see this as a cocktail type of place."

"Young lady, it's an anything you want type of place," Paul was looking directly at her now. Fixing his eyes onto hers. Definitely Michael's eyes, Alex could see them in her sleep.

"I am Chris." Alex knew now it was that type of place. No real names. But it would seem all old names that made Alex think of other people.

"I am Dee."

"D, just D?"

"Just Dee. Like just Madonna but shorter."

Paul took the beer from her hand and exchanged it with the cocktail that had just been made.

"Think this suits you better, I like to make sure your first time is special."

"What makes you think this is my first time" Paul laughed at Alex.

"It's your first time. This is my place."

"Your place? I thought this was a government place," Alex smiled back at him.

"This is my play paradise. I set all this up, provide the beer and the girls and the confidentiality. That is why I know you're a newbie. I must ask the question now though as a newbie, what is it you are actually looking for? Because you certainly have come dressed to impress." Alex needed to think quickly. She dressed as the ticket to get in. She hadn't really intended on going through with any of the activities on site. She was there to work. She was there to deal with Paul.

"Okay, I admit I am a newbie, so I need to know how all this works before I make up my mind on what to part take in, shall we say."

"Okay then bring your drink and I will give you the guided tour. It is the least I can do." Paul looked her up and down as if to appreciate what she had done for them by turning up dressed as she was.

All the time she was at the bar she could see James walking the floor with eyes always fixed on her. It was comforting to have another person in the room with you. Again, she thought back to Oliver. She would have preferred it was him looking over his shoulder at her. Alex followed Paul away from the bar with drink in hand.

"This is kind of the staging area. Green room if you like. Some call it the soft area if you want to come and just get down to business, one on one style, pretty straight then this is the place. Sometimes you might get a little girl on girl action, maybe?" Alex smiled at him. He was testing her preferences.

"The deeper you go the more the tastes change. A little further back over here a little S&M, there is some dominatrix work, you know for the person who wants a little spanking. Or ordering about." Suddenly Alex was surrounded by people, who were leather clad. Boots, skirts, one guy had a full rubber suit on with a gimp mask, all you could see was the lips from his mouth so that he could scream. There were various screams, but none in real pain. It was all about the pleasure for these weirdos.

"And the rooms at the back?" Paul was looking directly at her now.

"They are what I would say are for the more experienced. Not somewhere we get newbies very often." She almost felt like he was steering clear of them.

"Hey, I said I was a newbie here, not a newbie everywere." Alex could feel the word come off her tongue. She hadn't meant to say were, where, where she was saying it in her head over and over again.

"Everywhere is what I meant," Alex felt as if her mouth had lost some control. She kept rolling her tongue around it to bring it back to life.

"We can still look if you like?"

"I like," Alex had to concentrate to say the words. The drink that Paul had made her was obviously stronger than she had imagined.

In the first room there were two men and one woman. The woman was tied up in what looked like a harness. Currently upright and being softly whipped with a fluffy pink whip.

"Michelle here, she likes to be dominated and Andrew and Dan are obliging her fantasy. It starts off softly but trust me they do get a little more into it later and I am sure she will be rewarding the both of them before the night is over," Neither of them stopped to take notice of Paul.

The next room had stepped it up a bit. It was the same harness but with a man in there and two girls providing the torture. They weren't as gentle as Andrew and Dan. It was almost a flogging and there were traces of blood on the back of the man in the harness.

"Here you can see Stacey and Macy, I am sure they aren't their real names. Teaching Simon here a lesson in how to behave," Paul leant over and whispered to Alex.

"Believe it or not, Simon is the head of our primary school, takes all sorts newbie, all sorts."

Alex walked forward to the next room as she did her legs gave way.

"Careful," Paul caught her before she hit the ground

"Sorry don't know what has come over me," Alex had lost control of her bodily functions she was struggling to talk and to walk. The room had started to spin.

"It's okay, can be a bit intense on your first visit. Come sit down on the couch over there we can cool down a bit," Paul escorted her over to the couch. There were people on it, but as he approached they all managed to find somewhere else to go to carry on with their activities.

"That's better, so 'Just D' do you like what you have seen so far?" Alex was trying to concentrate her head was feeling fuzzy and she was having trouble focusing. This wasn't the drink. This was whatever he has put in the drink.

"I do, what did you put in my drink?"

"Me? Nothing however the barman has been known to add the odd loosener to a drink, to ensure everyone has a good time. Especially if it is your first time. Inhibitions can be bad for one's enjoyment."

Alex was trying to focus, she needed to see James and tell him to get her out of there. It was like she was moving in slow motion. So was everyone else. She continued to scan the room, but it was taking ages. She could hear Paul talking in the background to her but could only just make out the words.

"Drinks D?"

The same words were going over and over in her head. It was coming from Paul.

"Many drinks D." He was trying to speak to her but she didn't focus.

"How many?" Alex heard those words. Turned to look directly at Paul. She looked directly into his eyes but it wasn't Paul any more it was Michael Mellor.

"How many?"

Those words. Her words spoken back to her, again from him. Alex jumped back on the sofa but Michael kept coming forward.

"How many?"

He was still asking, Alex was still moving backwards she could not help thinking this was the longest couch in the world. The more she moved backward the more it felt as if there was further to go.

"How Many." Michael was looming over her. Those eyes that voice Michael was here again and he was going to get her, she knew it. She knew he was there for her.

"How many!" She got up and tripped backwards onto the floor. As she was down there she was almost trying to swim backwards to get away from him. The commotion alerted James to what was going on. He ran over.

"What's going on?" James was now between Paul and Alex. Alex focused for a second and then lost them both again.

"I am not really sure, think she has had one to many," James picked Alex off the floor. As he did Michael had gone and she could just about make James out.

"I will take her, she is my sister and came with me," There was a look from Paul. One of confusion. He had never heard of someone bringing their sister. Their girlfriend or wife at a push. But never a sister.

"I am sorry, your sister? Who are you?"

James already had Alex in his arms.

"We are just passing through, on base for a training session tomorrow and heard about this place," Paul just looked at him. He wasn't comfortable with the reply. James was built like a full blown soldier. He looked over at the man that had been guarding the door. He gave an agreeing nod as if to say they came together.

"Okay."

James carried Alex out of the hanger and into the car. He laid her on the back seat and drove off camp. At least there was some distance between them now. James drove to the end of the road and stopped the car. He went to the boot and fetched a few bottles of water and some chocolate. Sitting next to Alex he made her drink and eat. After about twenty-five minutes she started to come around.

"Are you okay? You have been out of it for a while."

"I think so, I am not sure what came over me."

"Paul did, one of the girls I was talking to was explaining to me that he does that with all the new girls. He likes to slip them something and then well slip them something. Sorry I didn't see you were in trouble till you got off the sofa and fell on the floor."

"That's okay, I didn't think I was, until that point," Alex lied she must have been getting clarity back. She was in trouble, she had been seeing Michael Mellor again. The guy was haunting her. The whole family had been.

"Where are we now?"

"Just outside the camp. I didn't think you would have wanted to leave fully. I thought you would have wanted to see if anything else happens," James was getting better at understanding Alex. That's exactly what Alex would want to do.

"Why don't you walk around and get some fresh air. I don't think that anyone is coming out of there anytime soon. The whole party was mid flow when we left."

Alex did just that. A walk in the fresh air did help. After about fifteen minutes she opened the back of the car and pulled out her black bag. It had clothes in there which she just put on top of the underwear she had been wearing. Her gun also. She was feeling safer by the minute.

"Thought you might like a cup of this?"

"Coffee?"

"Yes, coffee, I warmed it by using a heating stick and the cigarette lighter in the car," Alex took the coffee from him. He was right it was exactly what she needed.

"You are resourceful aren't you?"

"Not my first night out, have to be prepared,"

Alex and James sat in the car. Neither sure what they were waiting for, but it would start with the sight of a Ferrari roaring past them. It did, it was about three hours later but sure enough and Ferrari and a van past almost together. They followed. They followed as they went through the town to the 75 and then onto the 72 which meant they weren't going to the Grayling residence they were heading for the national park. Alex knew they had another one. Paul Grayling really didn't care about the locals or the police. This was his town and he would do as he pleased. Anyone else with this much heat on them would have just taken a body somewhere else to dispose of but not a Grayling.

As they entered the national park the van took a turn down a deserted track. Closely followed by the Ferrari and then by Alex and James. They held back as they saw the brake lights come on. Two men driving the van got out and went to the back doors opened it and pulled out a body.

Alex's theory had been right. The car hanger is where these people had been killed and they were using the National Park and the lake as dumping ground for the bodies.

"Time to go to work," James was under orders to stay in the car at all times and not to get involved. But that wasn't his style.

"Okay, what do you need me to do?"

"No, not you, I can handle this."

There was something about the way that Alex said that that made James believe it to be true.

Alex got out of the car and walked towards the Ferrari. Paul was still sitting in his car. The two men were unloading the body. Alex raised her gun and shot both of them square in the chest. If they were tied up enough in this to be dumping bodies in the woods, then they didn't deserve to go any further. Alex wasn't particularly interested in the henchmen she knew who the boss was. Paul was startled, and started his engine. Before he knew it his car door was open. And there was a gun at the side of his head.

"Get out."

Paul undid his seat belt and did what he was told. It wasn't until he was fully out of the car he recognised the person shouting the instructions.

"D, I knew there was something off about you, and your brother."

"The name is Alex, Chris, oh I mean Paul."

"You know who I am?"

"Yes I know who you are Paul Grayling," Paul almost relaxed at that point.

"Well if you know who I am then you know how much trouble you are in. This is my town." There was a cockiness to his swagger.

"This is my badge and I don't give a damn who you are." Alex pulled out her police badge. She really wasn't sure why she still carried it but it always got the same reaction. One of relief from the person she was dealing with, but she liked to feel disbelief also from her reactions around them.

"I own the police in this town."

"I have seen your sheriff, I am not surprised. But I am no normal police officer, Paul." Alex gestured over to the two men lying dead on the floor. At a second glance she could see that they were Andrew and Dan.

"Is that Michelle?" Paul Looked over and back at Alex. Alex had the flashback of Dan whipping her with the fluffy pink whip.

"Yes things just got out of hand. I was just helping them. They were the ones that took things a little too far."

"What with a pink fluffy whip?"

Paul didn't respond. He just continued to look directly at Alex.

"Things have got out of hand a lot over the last few months haven't they Paul?"

Again he didn't respond.

"How many times? A dozen is what I am being told?" Those words were ringing in Alex's head.

"How many?" As she said them the thought of Michael was back in her head again. He was looking at her and asking her how many Alex how many. Her eyes had obviously glazed over again at this point as this was Pauls chance to run at her. He did, she regained her focus really quickly. One shot in the leg had Paul on the floor. Screaming.

"You shot me!"

"I know, I told you I am not your ordinary police officer. Plus, you didn't answer my question Paul."

"But you shot me, police don't shoot first."

"I am special, Paul. Now back to my question before I shoot the other leg. How many?" Paul laid on the floor looking up at Alex.

"I have money."

"I have money too Paul, Let's be very clear I am not motivated by money. Just the truth and justice that is all. So, how many?" Alex's voice was getting louder. She wasn't concerned about anyone hearing them where they were. Even the gunshots were not going to be heard. Paul looked up.

"If I tell you, what happens next?"

Alex thought it was amazing that all people before they die always come up with the same lines. It wasn't me, I can buy you off, and let's make a deal.

"You tell me the truth and I will set you free."

"Really… just free."

"Free as much as you will be sentenced. Let's be very clear. We have the murder site. I have seen it, a team of forensics will tear that place apart and find the victim's blood everywhere. You have already confessed to being the boss, and here you are with a body, dumping it. You are hardly going to get away with anything are you? Confession will at least go as a plus point as you co-operated."

"Andrew and Dan are the ring leaders," he was still trying, the two dead men behind him. They were an easy culprit to blame.

"And?"

"And they get a little obsessive and don't know when to stop. I told them too, I really did but they just didn't listen."

"How many?"

"I don't know them all but I think they must have gone overboard at least ten times and dumped them in the lake." He was lying through his teeth. Alex knew it and he knew she knew it.

"Then they just got lazy did they? Started dumping the bodies on the road?"

"Yes that's why I said to them I would follow them, to ensure they didn't again," Paul was still grasping at his leg.

"What about Annabel?" Paul let go of his leg and moved backwards. That one was definitely his handy work. Alex had a theory that Paul had introduced them all to the darker side of sexual activity. He was the money and deviant behind everything.

"I am not sure who that is?"

"Don't lie to me Paul, else I will be aiming higher than the leg."

"I don't, I swear," Alex shot the ground next to him.

"Okay, okay it was all her, she wanted it harder and harder and I tried to tell her to stop, but she didn't want to, she enjoyed it too much. Before I knew it she was dead" Paul wasn't wincing in pain anymore. He was too focused on his lie.

"So if I am to believe you Paul. You are saying the dead guys behind you are the killers, Annabel was a sexual deviant who just took things too far and you are just a concerned citizen that wanted to ensure his friends didn't get caught for murder so drove out here to help them hide the body?"

Paul remained silent. Even he knew it was too hard to believe.

"I have money, as much as you want"

"Oh I forgot that, on top of it you want to pay off a police officer even though you haven't done anything?" Alex couldn't put up with the lies coming out of his mouth anymore.

"Okay."

She shot three times, leg stomach and then head. Just enough time in-between each shot so that he knew the pain of it, apart from the last.

She walked back to the car. James had sat and watched as it all went down. James waited for Alex to speak first.

"Fifteenish"

"Pardon?"

"The amount of people he has killed he reckons at least ten in the lake the other three and Michelle down there. He was lying all the time so who knows could be fifty for all we know." Alex was almost justifying her actions to James she didn't want him to feel that she had just got out of the car and executed these men.

"What do you want to do now?"

"Back to the hotel, let's clean up and get some rest. My head is still a little fuzzy from the drug he slipped me."

"He won't be doing that to anyone again will he?"

"I guess not."

James drove them back to the hotel. They parted company and agreed to meet for breakfast back at Spicy Bobs. Alex showered and laid on the bed. When she had been shopping in Flint she ensured her room had wine in it. So she poured herself a glass. And then another. It was thirty minutes of solid drinking before falling asleep. Again, she dreamt of Michael Mellor. Where ever she was, he was two steps behind her. She couldn't see him or touch him in her dream, but he was always there, always present. When she woke it was seven a.m. She had that nervous feeling that she couldn't remember what was real and what was the dream? She grabbed her gun and checked out the bathroom, nothing. Even opened the front door half expecting Michael to be on the other side. He wasn't, she began to focus again. Checking on the TV nothing about the events of last night. It was time to get out of town and get another case. Alex packed up and after checking out headed to Spicy Bobs.

She was there a good thirty minutes before James but waited for him to come before ordering.

"How are you this morning? How is the head?"

"Better thanks. Whatever that was last night in the drink sure packed a punch."

"Have you ordered?"

"No, I was waiting for you." The waitress walked across and they ordered. Again, not discussing anything else why she was near them.

"So where too next?" It was a good question and Alex hadn't really made up her mind. She knew she wanted another case as soon as possible. Whilst she was working she felt better more alive. The events of the week showed her that Christopher wasn't trying to kill her. James had been supportive and saved her. He didn't need to do that so maybe Mr Mellor was actually trying to clean up his mistakes. Was it that far-fetched an idea?

"I was thinking further west. I will find us a case. Unless that is you have anywhere else to be?" Alex posed the question to James. She knew little of him either.

"No, west is fine."

"No family, James? No one you need to be home for?"

"No, no family, Alex."

Just how Mr Mellor liked it she presumed. They all had loyalty but only to him. Alex was realising that she had now eaten more with James in a week than she had with Oliver in three months. Oliver had been thinking the same from the car down the road as he was still following close behind them. Even last night he had followed then into the national park. His rifle was aimed at Paul all the time and Oliver was ready to take him down should he have got the better of Alex.

Alex finished first and grabbed the newspaper from the side. The missing people and the Lake were on the front page but that wasn't the article that had Alex's attention.

Property tycoon Ian Stapleton sells portfolio to the Mellor Foundation.

Multi billionaire Ian Stapleton has announced today that he is selling his business to his lifelong friend and billionaire Christopher Mellor. Mr Stapleton who inherited a modest business from his father forty years ago has turned an annual profit of over £2 billion for the past five years. With a property portfolio that spans the globe.

Some say that his decision has been influenced by the fact that four days ago his only daughter Andrea Stapleton was killed in a car crash in her local town. Her parents are said to be devastated and want to now come out of the lime light and deal with their grief in private. Christopher Mellor said "This is a hard time for Ian and Sally, and my prayers are with them. I have done all I can to support them and their wishes for the future. This sale will ensure the future of their legacy that they tried to build for their daughter. Whilst giving them the time to deal with this awful tragedy."

Alex sat and read the article over and over again. Andrea Stapleton had been a killer, she knew as she killed her. How did they get the body out and into a car? There was even a picture of the car crash.

How many other instances that she caused had been covered up and spun a different story? Alex hadn't been looking backwards. She had only been looking at the next case.

Mr Mellor and Mr Stapleton. Lifelong friends she hadn't looked up who recommended the Stapleton's to the clinic as at the time she didn't have the files but she knew now. She knew it was going to be him. The initials IS that was next on her list. She had seen them in some documents, board papers or files. Was IS Ian Stapleton? Was he in on the Institute? There was a domino effect going on in Alex's mind. Everything was coming clear. She knew what Mr Mellor was doing and it was brilliant. There was a reason he had come from old money as he played the long game. Victoria Owens, she didn't stand a chance against him, he had sewn the whole thing up. Alex needed to stop him. She closed the newspaper. As calmly as she could she changed her plan.

"I have been thinking before we go west I need to go and see my parents?"

"Okay? Didn't you see them like a week and a bit ago?" James was still working his way through a huge stack of pancakes so wasn't really paying attention.

"I know but after three months radio silence I think I owe them another visit, besides, once we head west we don't know how many of these people we are going to find. Maybe a few months before we get back"

"Sounds sensible, but what is it, six, seven hours drive from here?" James looked at her as if to say really you want to make that journey. Alex nodded to him. She really did need to.

"Shall I Follow?"

"Yes if you want, do you know the address?"

"I do." Alex wasn't surprised at that.

"Probably a day tops if you want to book into the hotel down the road. I will stay for dinner tonight and we can set off sometime after breakfast tomorrow."

"Sounds like a plan," James didn't mind. He just continued eating.

Alex got up and paid for breakfast. She was in the car within five minutes hoping to lose James on route. He didn't even follow, he trusted she was going where she said she was. Alex was worried at the end of the road though. She noticed a black SUV just parked there with nobody in it. Nobody visible anyway. Oliver had seen her coming and ducked down. Alex knew that it was someone following her, either Mr Mellor or the president. The town's folk didn't have the money for eighty thousand dollar car. It would have been worth more than their houses.

She was going to have to be careful and watch over her shoulder to conclude what was coming.

Chapter Thirteen

Alex knew the drive was at least six and a half hours, eight and a half with the detour she needed to make. When she finally arrived at her parent's house it was dinner time. All the way down she was looking in and out of her mirror. Watching to see if anyone was following. They weren't. She took some back roads, just to make sure.

Oliver had met with James in the diner for a full update. He knew he was close behind after spotting him a few days ago on the stake out at the Graylings place, they spoke that night but James never told Alex he was close. Oliver was more concerned with Alex's wellbeing than anything else that had happened. He knew she could take care of herself, but he feared James wasn't the protector he should be for her. Oliver had genuine feelings for Alex, they were not just out of loyalty to Mr Mellor but also out of loyalty to Alex.

Alex rang ahead so wasn't surprised that when she arrived the whole family were coming to dinner.

"Hi mum."

"Hi honey we are so honoured, twice in almost a week." Alex's mum came up and hugged Alex as she walked in.

"I did promise mum, I can see you told everyone."

"Hey, not everyone, it's just your Father and Brother, Sandra and Ethan, they wanted to see you. It's been months since you have seen

Ethan." It had been. The last dinner they all had together was when Chris Masters was formally introduced to the family.

"I know, he looks like he gets taller every time I see him. Can't beat a good old family dinner." Alex walked through the kitchen and onto the porch. After a hug from each of them Jason had given the sign to Sandra to take Ethan inside.

"How is it Alex?"

"It's better dad. We have cleared quite a lot up, and things are better."

"Did you hear about the Curle farm Alex?" Even Alex didn't expect to get onto that conversation so quickly. It was almost as if he couldn't keep it in.

"Yes I did actually, the farm up the road, about thirty minutes away isn't it? I was reading about it in a diner, James was there wasn't he?" Alex struggled to look at either of them as she said it.

"Yes Alex apparently he had a hunch. I don't know you look at a guy on the force for twenty years, and never knew he had one in him."

Alex knew her father didn't believe James was a good cop. At least not good enough to resolve that case on his own. The look in his eyes said you know more than you are telling, Alex. Alex didn't look back at him.

"The day you left as well?"

"Really dad? I didn't know," She turned her shoulder to him to speak to Jason. Almost as a permanent stop to the conversation.

"How are Sandra and Ethan, where did they go?"

"They are great Alex, they promised they would help mum with dinner." She knew it was a lie and that they wanted her on her own.

"I swear that boy gets bigger every week, how is he getting on at school?" There was a silence. Alex knew they had questions and whilst she felt closer than ever in resolving all of this she didn't want them involved in the answers.

"School is good, got into the soccer team which is great news." Silence again.

"Is it nearly over Alex?"

She thought for a moment. She really believed it was. For the first time she had clarity in what was going on. She had a plan formulating in her head in order to bring this to a conclusion well at least to bring it to such a conclusion she could hand it all over to Victoria Owens. One meeting with Victoria had her convinced that you needed to fight power with power. If anyone could handle Mr Mellor it was her.

"I think it is dad. In fact I am going to be heading up to Washington tomorrow to see if I can get this resolved"

"Washington Alex? Not to the big house?"

"Think so Jason, as I said this thing that I am involved in. It goes straight to the top. I met with Victoria Owens not a week ago," Alex hadn't lied to them about that. She didn't include the part to say that the president of the United States drugged and kidnapped me. But a meeting is a meeting.

"Really Alex, part of the big dinner eh?"

"Something like that."

The other thing that Alex had read in the paper was that the world trade summit was being held in Washington tomorrow. All the countries were attending and it was sponsored by none other than the Mellor Foundation. Christopher Mellor was going to be there. More importantly, Stephen Henderson's father was going to be there also. Alex had unfished business with his son and her plan was going to have to involve getting Mr Mellor out of his comfort zone.

"Shall we eat?" Sandra came out onto the porch.

"Hey Sandra, what do you think of my little sister eh, met the president last week, and heading to the White House tomorrow." Jason was proud of what he believed his little sister to be doing.

"Really Alex that's amazing. I voted for her."

"Think the whole country voted for her."

"I know, don't tell mum though, else I will be down town first thing in the morning buying the right dress with the right shoes."

"Come on you lot, dinner." Alex's mum appeared from the kitchen , it was great timing for Alex. She knew the rule no work talk at the dinner table. For the second time in a fortnight Alex loved the fact that she was back home. For Alex it felt like the safest place in the world. Work talk died down, and they were back to the important conversations. Like Ethan's school, how skinny Alex was and whether or not she was ever going to get another date.

It slipped out about the White House and her mother had a million ideas on who she should or should not be looking out for. From movie stars to politicians, Alex got the low down on who would be suitable for her. That was what dinner with the family was like, someone was always the brunt of the conversation whilst they sat and ate for a few hours. Her father would always ensure they had enough wine with at the dinner table to make it a lengthy evening. At the end of dinner, Alex had to front a few questions from her father over a brandy on the porch. But that was just the two of them. She did promise that she wasn't the the Real Avenger's as he had put it. It was just too much of a coincidence for him that she was there when the Curle farm case was solved.

Her father was a good captain and a better cop. As long as she was safe that was the main thing for him. He knew she was strong but that was still his little girl out fighting crime. Alex said her goodnights and went to sleep in her old room. They had had a couple of glasses of wine with dinner but not enough to put Alex to sleep straight away. She lay on the bed thinking about Christopher, where she thought all of this had come from and where it was going to end. Michael was still there too. The constant figure in her thoughts. It was as if she couldn't forget his blue eyes, and silky voice they were haunting her days and nights. Her dreams were of Michael and Maria. She must have woken herself half a dozen times in the night but each time she fell back to sleep, it was to dream of the Mellor's. Alex woke as her father came into the room.

"Hey Dad."

"Hey, didn't mean to wake you."

"I know, I needed to get up soon anyway, promised mum I would go to the market with her. Market only, no dress shopping."

"Good luck with that princess, you know what she is like once she starts." Her dad leaned over her and kissed her on the forehead.

"Be careful in Washington Alex, and come home soon."

"I will, I promise," Alex turned over as if to go back to sleep.

Her father left the room. She laid back on the bed. Alex believed there to be a sense of danger in what was coming. Taking her mother shopping meant maybe putting her in danger. Never knowing who was watching and from where. Alex spent a few minutes convincing herself it was safe. They weren't going to come after her. Not yet anyway.

Alex was ready to challenge Mr Mellor, clearly one of the most powerful men on the planet. In order to assist one of the most powerful women on the planet. A morning at the market would ease her mother, and take her mind off things.

After breakfast, Alex and her mum set out to the market. This was a regular fortnight thing for them before Jack's death. Alex didn't shop but her mum did, Alex had no need, her diet consisted of takeaways and wine three months ago and today it was hotel food and wine. There had been very little cooking going on for quite a while. They pulled up outside and went into the indoor market. The stalls were full of people selling vegetables, meat, fish, and nick nacks of all kinds. Her mother loved this place. Always taking the same walk up and down in the same order and stopping for a coffee half way around. Alex felt like she was home. Her mother chatted with each of the stall owners and in turn they were all happy to see Alex.

"Alex?"

Alex turned, Chris Masters was standing in front of her. It almost took her breath away. Her mother turned at the same time. She spoke first.

"Hi Chris."

"Mrs Keaton," Chris was looking directly at Alex.

"Chris."

Alex was stuck for words. She hadn't expected this. She didn't really have a plan to talk to him. She led with a hug and a kiss. He responded but almost instantly pushed her away.

"Can we talk Alex?"

Alex looked at her mum, she nodded her head. She had no intent on saving her from him. Chris had been calling the house almost daily for the past three months looking for Alex. Her mum knew how much Alex had meant to him. Alex did give her mother the look to see if this had been set up. She wasn't sure.

"Yes sure, let's get a coffee. Mum I will meet you in the middle."

Alex showed Chris the way to the coffee shop. She didn't speak all the way there. And went to the counter and bought two coffees. Bringing them over to where Chris was sitting. They looked at each as they sat down. Time seemed to freeze for just a moment.

"I am not really sure where to start Chris."

"Me neither Alex, I almost crashed the car when I saw you pass by with your mother. I didn't even know you were back in town."

"I am not, I am just passing through and I am sorry I haven't called."

"How long have you been back?"

"I have just come to visit my parents. Arrived late last night. I haven't done that in three months. Or spoken with them, figure I owed my mother some one on one shopping time." Alex knew that her father and brother weren't going to mention the one other visit they had had. Alex wasn't one hundred per cent sure he believed her.

"Think you owe me a visit Alex?" Alex wasn't sure that she did. They weren't married, they weren't really a real couple. They had just been friends who slept together. Well that was Alex's view. She didn't respond.

"Why Alex?" Why was a big question? Why haven't you called, why have you abandoned me, why haven't you been to your parents or work. Alex knew he would want the answers to all those questions.

"I got caught up in something, I still am. I am just taking a moment out to remember why I am doing this. That is why I am here." Alex didn't want to look him in the eye.

"Caught up in something? Is it to do with the Mellor's? The Institute? I followed your passport and the English press and the events around Michael Mellor? Was that all you? Did your theories pan out?"

"Was what me?" Alex was keen to ignore the last question.

"The false suicide?"

"The what?"

"Dr Smith, at first they thought that he had committed suicide after shooting Michael Mellor. They now believe that there was another party involved. Something to do maybe with a download of files from the institute about nine months ago."

Alex stayed quiet.

"You know Alex the files, these files," Chris produced the hard drive that Dee had given him.

"Where did you get that?"

"Dee, before she passed them to you she copied them onto her computer. We met with her three months ago" Alex knew she had made a copy of the list. Dee hadn't mentioned giving a copy to Chris.

"What is going on with these Alex?"

"I need you to give me that Chris, I can't tell you why, not yet but you can't have a copy of those files they are really dangerous?"

"Dangerous how Alex? because it has the names of a hundred thousand patients that may or may not be killers?"

"Who else knows you have these files Chris?"

He paused for a moment.

"Nobody other than me and James."

"You swear?"

"Yes I swear, when we couldn't get hold of you we decided to keep it that way until your return Alex." Chris was still holding the device. He looked genuine in what he was saying. She knew they were both out to protect Alex as much as they could.

"Are you coming home Alex?"

"I am, I mean I will be as soon as we can get this cleared up."

"And then what about us?" Alex wasn't convinced there was an us. There was sex. But nothing else. He wasn't going to let this go. She had only been with one man with whom she felt a real connection, and that was Oliver. And today she had banished him away from her.

"We need to see when I get back." She knew in her heart what would happen but she needed that hard drive away from him. It was for his own good. As she took it out of his hand the smell of blood hit her nostrils.

Chris's body hit the table in front of her. A single shot had hit the side of his head. It must have been from some distance and with a silencer. Because there was hardly a sound. Alex heard the scream of the person next to her before she could react. She grabbed the hard drive and just ran. Not to her mother but out of the market and into the street. She wasn't sure if the bullet had been meant for her or for him but she wasn't taking a chance to find out. Her mum and dad would be better off if she wasn't around so that is what she intended to do.

She flagged down the nearest cab and headed back to the house. Picked up her car and got on the road.

Oliver was on the phone when he left the Market place.

"Yes sir, it would seem she gave the second hard drive to one of her old colleagues. Yes, sir, that's all of them, other than the ones she is carrying. I could not make out the whole conversation but Dr Masters and her partner James were the only two others who knew about it. I will take care of her ex-partner now and meet you in Washington sir"

Oliver put the rifle case in the car and drove to the local police station to deal with James.

Chapter Fourteen

Alex picked up her phone and rang Mr Mellor's James when she was about half an hour away from town. She wanted to make sure there was distance between her and her family before she did.

He sounded calm, not like he had just killed someone in cold blood. Alex couldn't really tell either way, but they agreed to meet in Washington. It was only an hour drive for them in total so they would be there by lunch time with plenty of time to put a plan together. Alex needed the Mellor's to think everything was normal.

The World Trade conference dinner was at the White House but Alex wasn't so much bothered about that. She was more interested in finding Stephen Henderson. There had been a score to settle with him. Alex didn't like unfinished business.

After the events in New York it was clear that Stephen's father didn't trust him to stay there anymore. Alex had been watching him over the last week whilst she was waiting for Mr Grayling to make his move. Most of the time his tracker had him placed in a rented house in Hyattsville. Rented by his father as it was close to the White House. It over looked the Ancostia River. As bright as his father was, Alex had wondered why he would put him in a place where temptation and opportunity would be in his grasp. The river had been surrounded by local footpaths and woods and was easy stalking ground for someone like Stephen.

Alex found a hotel not too far from the river. It was a step up from the one in Grayling and even had a minibar in the fridge. The World Trade conference dinner had been for dignitaries only. Stephens's father and mother would be attending and that made Alex believe that if there was a night he was going to play up. Then tonight was it.

Alex left a message on James's phone to tell him that she had found a case and that they were to be ready in the lobby of the hotel for about six p.m.

James was waiting for her when she arrived.

"Where are we going?"

"It's not far, should be a pretty easy case. One guy, killed a couple of girls and hurt a few more. Think he will attack again tonight so time is of the essence."

"Are we car sharing then?"

"No, you take yours, I may need to go somewhere afterwards." Alex didn't want to travel with him. Not tonight.

James followed Alex the short journey into Hyattsville. They parked overlooking the river. There were a number of houses backing onto it, with a foot path either side of the river. Popular for dog walkers and people alike. Both footpaths were tree lined which concerned Alex. Visibility was key to be able to see what Stephen was up too.

She knew which house he was in. She also knew his security team would be walking around the house. At least at the back and along the river. If his father knew what he was, his security surely would as well. They would be protecting him from himself.

Alex's plan was to wait outside for him to make his move. His father will have left for the dinner by six, and she knew Stephen would be itching for a fix anytime soon. She was going to give him till around eleven p.m., if he hadn't made his move by then she was going to have to make one of her own.

9.47 p.m. she didn't have to wait long to get her first site of Stephen. He was in the back garden. Pacing up and down on the phone.

He looked busy, mid conversation. Clearly knowing his security's movements as almost as the guard went out of site at the back of the fence Stephen had jumped it. Alex sat and waited for him to come out of the bushes on the other side but he didn't, she waited a while longer and still nothing.

The security guard had done another full circuit of the perimeter and he still hadn't moved. She was about to go down there and see if there was another way out that she couldn't see, when he appeared.

He appeared just as there was a young lady walking past, as quickly as he came out of the bushes he was back in. This time with a woman. He walked up behind her and hit her over the head. Knocking her unconscious. Alex was out of the car before she saw him push her over the fence and back onto the property. He dragged her into the house.

It was better than she could have expected. She had him and a victim, and a witness. Her plan would work even better now.

Alex returned to the back of the car pulling out her black bag.

"Alex."

James was behind her. She didn't respond.

"Alex." He spun her round and her gun was in his side before she was stood facing him.

"Can I help you James?" James could feel the gun digging into his ribs.

"He is off limits you know this Alex." Whilst they both knew Alex had the better of him in this situation. James still sounded forceful in his statement.

"I know you have said he is off limits, but let's be clear James nobody is off limits when we are talking about this."

"I can't let you Alex." There was a tone to his voice to tell Alex this wasn't going to end well if she carried on.

"I am not asking James, take your gun out now," Alex pushed her gun closer into his side. James did as he was told. He took it out and held it out.

"Now toss it to the river." James did as he was told.

"Sorry." Alex shot him straight in the thigh James screamed and held his arms down to it. At the same time Alex swung and knocked him around the top of the head. It put him out cold on the floor. Alex wasn't pulling her punches.

She turned back to her bag took out some cable ties and tied his hands together and feet and dragged him towards his own car. She also pulled out a bandage and wrapped around his thigh. James had probably saved her life back at camp Grayling, she didn't want to shoot him but there was a bigger picture at play here. Whilst she couldn't prove it, she did feel that James had killed Chris. It made shooting him easier. James and her family were the only ones who knew where she was. It wasn't a coincidence that someone happened to stumble on Chris and Alex having coffee. Alex had tried to watch her back but it was coming all too clear, there were too many people following her that she couldn't see.

Alex went back to her bag, made sure everything was in there. Her hard drive and the one from Chris. She took the tracker and the fingerprint too. If everything went to plan she would be handing all this over to Victoria Owens. Alex took out her phone to ensure it had full battery. It did. She closed the car, checked on James and then walked down to the river.

When Alex arrived behind the house she followed the same route into the house that Stephen had taken. The patio doors were still open although she couldn't hear any screams for help. On arrival she could see Stephen in the living room undressing the girl. She still looked unconscious. There had been no movement from her.

Alex slid the doors open and crept into the room.

"Stephen, stop what you are doing, and move away."

Stephen was shocked to hear the voice. He had always half expected to be caught, but not by a woman, and not by one he recognised instantaneously.

"Wait, you are?"

"I am well aware who I am Stephen. Just stop what you are doing and back up."

Stephen stopped and sat back against the couch, with the unconscious woman still lying next to him.

"I presumed my father must have paid you off? How did you find me?"

"As I mentioned before Stephen, money means nothing to me and you're not hard to track, Stephen, now are you? Hardly an unknown face in the crowd."

"But this is my house. I just have to scream and there will be security in here in seconds."

"Why would you do that? When you were about to have your fun. Plus, I can be out of here as quickly as you were when you captured her. After shooting you of course." Alex needed Stephen as part of the plan.

"So what now? Going to arrest me? We have been here before. Detective Alex Keaton," That did take Alex back a bit. He now knew who she was.

"Been doing your homework have you Stephen?"

"No, my father has though. He told me about you." There was an almost smug look on his face as he said that.

"Really what did he say?"

"He said you weren't going to be an issue anymore and you worked for the board." The board those words were stuck in her head. Was Stephens's dad on the board also? Would make sense if they came from money and have the influence and power of the senate. That is Mr Mellor's inner circle of friends.

"Well let's just say that I am about to give my notice to the board. And no I don't want to arrest you. All I need you to do is place a call to your father. Nothing more. I can then handle the rest from there?"

"My father? Is that what all this is about? Is he behind you stalking me?" Alex shook her head back at Stephen.

"No, that is not what it's about. But I need you to give him a message. Take out your phone and dial him."

Stephen did what he was told. He had lost respect for his father years ago and anything that would help upset him, Stephen had a desire to do.

"What do you want me to say to the prick?"

"Here read this to him."

Alex handed over a piece of paper.

"Dad, just listen. I am in Hyattsville with Mrs Brown from the Institute. She said that Christopher Mellor would want to know that. Tell him that she would like a word. If you don't tell him, we are going for a small walk into the park together. And this time there will be no one to rescue me."

There was no response. The secretary of state just hung up on his son.

"What did he say?"

"Nothing he just hung up, was that all you wanted? Or are we really going for a walk in the park?" Alex didn't respond to his question.

"Now we just wait here. Do you believe your father will want to save you?"

"I believe he will want to keep any scandal out of the press and if that means saving me, then yes."

It was time to stage the scene, Alex closed all the doors and curtains to the room. You couldn't see in or out. She then cable tied both Stephen and the girl and placed them on the couch.

Then she turned the heating up using the thermostat and sat next to them. She was in no doubt that the secretary of state and Mr Mellor would call Stephen's own detail first to check if it was true. They had, and his detail reported back the situation. There was no sound from the house everything was locked and all the curtains had just been closed.

Alex was worried what equipment they had outside, heat seeking rifles was something she thought of first. By sitting on the couch she hoped that the signature wouldn't be clear. She needed Christopher Mellor there for her plan to work.

It was the World Trade dinner, it wasn't going to be a quick turnaround. Christopher couldn't just walk out of it. Alex knew that. It took a little over two hours before she heard a familiar voice at the door.

"Alex, Alex." It was Oliver's voice she recognised.

"Yes Oliver," Alex moved over to behind the door.

"Are you going to let us come in?"

"That depends Oliver, who is us?"

"It's just me and Christopher, Alex? We just want to talk."

Alex walked over and unlocked the front door.

She walked backwards to the couch with her gun straight out in front.

"Slowly."

They both entered to room.

"Mr Henderson, I am so glad to see you alive. I must say I thought the worst on the car trip over."

"Mr Mellor, please take a seat next to the young passed out lady."

Christopher did as he was told.

"Oliver, where I can see you. Standing in that corner will be fine." Oliver did as he was told also. With a smile on his face. It was good to see Alex and he felt a slight sense of pride that she was going to take the fight to them. He had expected it to happen at some point.

"Where is my father?"

"Your father isn't coming son, the message was for me, and it was heard loud and clear." Christopher turned his attention back to Alex.

"Good I am glad it was. I want some truths Christopher. I want to know exactly what has been going on. Not the spin you gave Maria," Christopher looked directly at Alex without losing eye contact.

"Alex, why don't you tell me what you think is going on, clearly that's why you have brought me here and by all accounts needed a bargaining chip? So you took this poor man and what I can only presume his girlfriend hostage?"

Alex looked at back at him. She didn't really want to start it the conversation as a lot of it was still hypothetical and in her head. Spilling it all would give him an opportunity to change his story. And if she was wrong she only had one go at this.

"Andrea Stapleton?"

"Andrea, is that who this is about. Andrea, it was a tragic accident. Her parents are heartbroken about it." Everything Christopher was saying he did so with a smile on his face.

"You know it wasn't an accident Christopher, you know what happened."

"I am sorry what do you mean Alex?" The tone in his voice felt like she was being accused of something. She felt like she was the one in the wrong for even asking him about it.

"You know, don't lie, you covered up what happened in order to get your claws into her father's company, that's when it hit me, I was thinking about all of this wrongly. I thought you were out to create something, splice the gene pool, create the ultimate murderer or something, when all along, this whole thing has been down to the basics, it is all about power and money isn't it? That's why Stephen here, he is one as well isn't he. What did his family come from, money, educated in Harvard or Princeton something like that? You knew that these kids were growing up to be prominent figures in society and you could use that, you could use that for power money and influence over the people who we deem above the law."

Christopher's face changed it wasn't a smirk anymore. He sat back.

"Wow, that is quite a story but I honestly can't say I know what you are talking about?"

"You know what I am talking about Christopher." Christopher just sat with a blank look on his face. It was making Alex mad.

"I really don't my dear?"

"About the Brown Institute, about the fact you're the funder, about the fact that all these people have the DNA of a murderer or psychopath in them. Like your son Michael, Andrea, Deacon," Christopher still sat there no acknowledgment to what she was saying.

"Alex I am part of this elaborate story? My son was one of them too? What, a murderer? I am led to believe he was killed in Germany after a date with the daughter of a dear friend of mine? Another tragic event Alex. I really think you may need some help." Alex was getting even more wound up with his responses.

"You are the cog in the centre of it Mr Mellor. If you weren't prominent in the whole affair, then why isn't his father here instead of you? I wouldn't be surprised if you included your son in the development so you knew it was working, so that you knew you were getting value for your money. It's your name that is coming up over and over again with the international policy commission, the treasury, the foreign policy all of them over and over again. Not including all the oil and technology deals that have passed hands in the last few years." Alex was really trying her luck with that statement all she really knew is what the President had told her. If he pushed her on what policy what deal she didn't have a clue.

"You see I am not the only one looking into you Christopher so is Victoria, you know Victoria Owens the President of the United States. Yes, we have met and she is looking into you also. She knows about your little board."

Christopher Mellor's face had turned serious. Alex was playing poker with little more than a pair of twos but the bluffing seemed to have the desired effect.

"When did you meet Victoria, Alex? The president of the United States is part of this crazy idea of yours is she?" Christopher was now looking at Oliver. He wasn't acknowledging Alex's rant but with that statement he was uncomfortable. What if he had been betrayed by his own people?

"We met just before Oliver and James came to collect me from the hotel. You know the hotel that I stayed in the night that I killed Andrea Stapleton. I don't know how you found her, or managed to spin it, but I killed her because she had killed two others and that's how I know you covered it up." This had Christopher rattled.

"We met, we had a little conversation about you and what you were up to."

Christopher stood up.

"Sit down." Alex wasn't playing she had the gun directly sighted on him. Christopher slowly sat down.

"Listen Alex, I am unsure what you are trying to say here, that you're a murderer? Andrea Stapleton died in a car crash. You may be having a little bit of a breakdown and we need to get you some help and soon."

"You are the murderer Mr Mellor. I presume it was you that shot my friend in the market place this morning?"

"I am sorry Alex I don't know what you mean," he wasn't going to be caught out by the trap. Alex had her phone running on record on the table behind the sofa. Whatever he was going to say it wasn't going to be a confession. This was making Alex mad. Her rage was hard to control.

"Besides I think you will find Alex that you are in fact the main suspect in that shooting. It's why I rushed straight over here. I was worried about you after you saved my son. Imagine my shock when I heard the news not an hour ago."

"What news?"

"The news. Apparently there was a shooting in a market place. A dozen eye witnesses have a young woman in her thirty's receiving a black box device from a young man. Standing up and shooting him in the head. It's believed the couple have a history of turmoil in their relationship. It is believed, I want to say Chris Masters hit her and she has been previously on the run from him for the last three months. He really was looking for her, calling police stations nationwide, week by week. Obsession I think they called it. They meet and you, well a girl very similar to you, killed him," Alex stood looking directly at him. He had spun this to the news. He probably had the news stations in his pockets also.

"What have you done?"

"Me Alex, nothing" There was a smile on his face. Alex was close to shooting him just to wipe it off. Killing him would have been a great relief but it wouldn't give her what she needed.

"Now how do you want to play this Alex? I am sure this unconscious woman and Stephen here are willing to forgive you bursting into their home and interrupting their date. Oliver and I forgive you for calling us out of our dinner and let's get you some help Alex? Maybe even get you back to work? You love your work don't you? You want to get back to it don't you? There has been no real harm here. Other than to James one of my security detail, who thanks by the way, is on his way to the hospital with a gunshot wound. What do you say? Forget it all happened."

Alex didn't know what to do. He wasn't going to bite he was calm and collective she couldn't get him wound up to spill the truth.

"Just pass the gun to Oliver and we will just get this whole thing cleaned up," Alex's blood started to boil. He was again out smarting her. He had the power he had the money she wasn't going to get him to admit to anything. She had nothing on him.

"This isn't over Mr Mellor, I know what you are." Alex started to walk towards Oliver.

"I am sure it isn't Alex. Let's just call it a bad day. You go home and I will ensure someone visits you to help you through this troubled time. I can then go back to the White House and explain to the secretary of state that his son is fine and well and it was all a big misunderstanding."

Alex held the gun out towards Oliver, as he reached for it she spun and shot Stephen Henderson straight in the head and the girl next to him. Christopher Mellor jumped backwards off the couch for fear of being next.

Oliver lifted his hand and knocked Alex to the floor, she was out cold.

Chapter Fifteen

Alex was out cold for about twenty minutes. Oliver had pulled his punch when he hit her across the side of the head. It was Oliver who revived her but under Mr Mellor's instructions.

"Alex."

"Alex."

She started to stir, de ja vu was taking place. It felt so similar to the stable at the Curle farm but this time it was Oliver who knocked her out.

"Get off," Alex pushed his hand away and moved back. She remembered where she was and she was looking for her gun. Christopher Mellor had it in his hand.

"You knocked me out?" Alex's look at Oliver was making him feel guilty.

"I know, I had to."

"You had to?"

"I had to Alex, If I hadn't of taken you down the people outside would have." Oliver pointed to the radio in his ear. And opened his jacket to show a silver shield on the inside pocket. Her first assumptions about heat seeking equipment had been correct. Both he and Christopher were tagged so they could show the guys outside with rifles where they were in the house.

"This is a very touching reunion but it has to end." Christopher was interrupting.

"He may have saved you from the guys outside, Alex but never the less you will not be leaving here today. Stephen may have been a psychopathic murderer Alex, but he was the secretary of state's son and you will have to die for that." Alex looked up at Christopher he had her gun in one hand and her phone in the other. It was the first time she had heard a clear threat from him.

"That was the plan then was it, Alex for you to lure me here, get me to confess all to you and you were going to pass the recording on to Victoria? Or was that all a lie, have you actually even met her?"

Alex sat and looked at him. It was over as he said, she wasn't going to get out of this room. It was the risk she took. She had planned and known there was a likeliness that only one of them was leaving.

"If this is it? Then why don't we both confess all. I think we owe each other that. After everything we have been through," Alex gestured that she wanted to get up. Christopher nodded. She sat on the couch next to the other two bodies. Christopher pulled up a chair and sat in front of her face to face Oliver remained standing in the corner.

"I think you should start Christopher. I think you owe me that just for what I have been trying to do for you?" Christopher nodded.

"Okay, I am sorry it has come to this Alex as I was really starting to like you, I just wanted you to know that." Christopher paused.

"At first I honestly didn't know the secrets of the Brown Institutes. I genuinely took Carly on the two-year trip to Europe to look at having a baby. When they explained to us we were pregnant, and it was twins you can imagine how excited we would had been. First it seemed like a normal childhood. Looking back though I think I always knew he had a temper. It was hard to control him. We went through a dozen nannies from four till ten years old and after that we struggled to get anyone to look after him. At eleven, after an incident with the hunting dogs and a knife, I took him back to Paris. I wanted some tests. They wanted some donations. I set about investigating the place. My private detectives are very thorough, about three weeks later I knew chapter and verse."

"And at that point you didn't close it down? What kind of father are you?" Christopher ignored the question.

"Something from you now Alex. Did you really meet Victoria Owens?"

Alex thought hard about lying to him. She didn't owe him anything. But then she also knew she wasn't leaving the room. If this was the end she really did need to know the truth.

"I did, just as I said. Although they drugged and kidnapped me to get me there. I thought it was you. When she came into the room, I was shocked."

"What did she say Alex?"

"No not yet. I have one short story to tell, I need more from you first."

Christopher nodded. He had resigned himself to tell her everything as she was about to die.

"I found who their financial backers were and cut off their money supply until they agreed to meet with me. I made them tell me everything. I was shocked, I will be honest. Once I calmed down I did ask about a cure. They assured me there was no such thing. I spent a couple of days contemplating what to do next. It was a tough choice. My heart said pull it down brick by brick. My head said that I had referred maybe fifty couples to the Institute. Friends, family and colleagues. I called another board meeting with all of them and asked for all of my recommendations files. Almost all of them were going through the same as I was. Mostly boys, and all psychopaths and murderers. They explained to me that when Michael and the others hit puberty it was going to get a lot worse."

"And you saw an opportunity in that?"

"I thought that I could turn it into my advantage I will not lie. When I left the room I was the major investor and the new chairman of the board. I hadn't left them any other option."

There was a moment's silence. Some relief from Alex that her thoughts had been correct. He was the main cog in the wheel. From Christopher a remembrance of finding out his now dead son was a natural born killer.

"Victoria, Alex," Christopher had shared enough for now.

"She wanted to know what our relationship was. She had been following Stephen privately, she knew about the park and the girls and she wanted to know why you would kidnap the victim of an attack and take her to your hotel?"

"That is all?" Christopher looked surprised.

"Who are the board?"

"Was that all?"

"Who are the board?" Christopher knew how stubborn she could be so there was no point trying to argue with her. The sooner this was done the sooner he would know his next steps.

"I had done most of the damage already with my recommendations. You would be surprised how many men needed help in that department, Alex. Especially men with money who marry girl's half their age. It wasn't just IVF treatments, there were fertility drugs, new ovaries, our technology and research was developing. The institutes are a profitable business, Alex, and not just the treatments were paying off. Knowing what these people were going through, knowing what some of our children had done. Was turning profitable also."

"Blackmailing your friends?"

"Blackmail is an ugly word; Alex I like to think what I was doing was protecting them against bad publicity"

"What about the trackers?"

"My idea, I had genuinely purchased them for my children. One to protect Maria and another to ensure I knew where Michael was at all times. These things are hardly traceable now. We inject a tracker directly into the blood. It's why we could go back and ensure that every child leaving the facility was fitted or retro fitted with a tracker."

"So I was right, it was all a power and money thing." Christopher paused.

"It's what I do Alex. Victoria?"

"She asked me about the hotel. Stephen Henderson and the Institute."

"She knows about the institute?"

"Did you kill Chris?"

"Alex she knows about Germany?" This did concern Christopher Mellor.

"Did you Kill Chris?"

Trying to bargain with a dead woman was never going to work. She knew her days were up what did she have to lose other than to be stubborn.

"Yes, but you gave us no choice Alex. We knew how many copies you had made and we knew you kept two for yourself we just didn't know where it was. We listened in and he mentioned only he and one other knew about the files so to keep this from falling in the wrong hands they had to go and quickly."

"James you killed James as well. What is up with you?" Alex was on her feet and screaming.

"Sit down Alex," It was Christopher's turn to point the gun directly at her.

"Yes I am sorry Alex. I warned you nobody else can know about this. If you had kept it to yourself this would have just carried on. If truth be known, the board for a while have been requesting a clear up mission of all the old cases and what you were doing was helping alleviate that pressure for me."

Alex was still trying to come to terms with the fact that both James and Chris were gone, because of her, and her quest for the truth. But mostly because of Mr Mellor. The hatred was boiling up inside her for him.

"You didn't need to kill them!"

"You didn't need to tell them," Alex suddenly thought about her family. Her brother and father. If they were listening in on that conversation what else were they listening in on? Had she slipped up with them?

"My family?" Alex's voice was softer She didn't really want to hear an answer.

"They are fine Alex. I don't believe you told them anything. And it was a good job that Oliver stopped the post. Even I didn't know he had done that till he brought the packages to me." Alex looked over at Oliver who hadn't moved or said anything during this whole time. He had been protecting her. If it weren't for him her family would have been dead also.

"Victoria, Alex I am being more than fair"

"I was tied to a chair and questioned. About all of it. I said I was just in the wrong place at the wrong time. I had had my difficulties with your son. And you were worried that I was looking into you. Let's face it she was, so it was the right thing to say. Wait a fucking minute did you say institutes!" Alex was relaying the Q&A session in her head and it just came to her. At least twice he had said institutes and that they were turning a profit.

"Did you mean Paris and Germany?"

Christopher sat back in the chair. Clearly Alex didn't know about that. And If Alex didn't know the president didn't know either. Germany was the only one they were looking into. This was great news for Christopher.

"Yes Alex institutes. It's been twenty years Alex did you not think that I would be building on a successful business?" The thought hadn't even crossed her mind. She thought that it was in Paris so it was so far away that he wouldn't be associated with it. When she had done her research on the Brown Institute shortly after Jack had died she didn't find more than one?

"How many?" Those words again coming out of Alex's mouth. They weren't this time asking how many people have you killed. They were asking how many Murder factories have you created.

"Thanks to Mr Stapleton and his portfolio of property Alex I believe there are eleven world-wide. Paris was the first and we were moving to Germany. Anyway we needed bigger premises it just looked to you like we had done it because of the break in. Europe's population continues to exploded and due to some of their let's say poor diets, especially in the UK. They are needing more and more assistance in conceiving a child and that is where we come in."

Eleven Brown institute's, Alex hadn't expected this. She hadn't even thought it was possible. What else had they been doing there, testing there, and creating there?

"And the closing of the one in Germany?"

"I leaked the press release. We weren't sure we were going to close. But now you have confirmed to me it's the only one the president knows about then it will close. I will ensure we come up with a story for her after the funeral obviously, of the secretary of state's son. So what else does she know?" Alex was a little dazed and confused. She thought she knew the quest she had been on. She read the files and watched the dots on the tracker every night. They had been calling her to come and get them. But that was just one branch of the chain. This thing was global. All she could think about was work. She needed to work even more now. The thought of that many killers out in the world made her sick to the stomach. She could feel herself tensing up.

"Victoria, nothing more. That's why it is silly to kill me Mr Mellor. I can continue on now, now I know everything?" Alex was making a plea for her life. Because she knew she wanted to finish this. Christopher looked at her straight in the eyes.

"Are you sure she knows nothing?"

"Nothing, she knows nothing. As I said I told her I was at the wrong place at the wrong time." Christopher believed her. Alex was in as much trouble as he was if this got out. She had murdered scores of people in the last three months.

"I just want to go back to work Mr Mellor. Even more so given what we have discussed. If what I was working on was only one branch of the empire, then how good do you think it will sit with your board that we can help clear up everything else." Christopher was sitting back in his chair again.

"You want to go back to work?" Alex felt that was almost an offer and pounced on it.

"Yes, very much so. I know I can help you and now I know the truth, I am not going to be looking for that. All I am going to be doing is solving cases."

Again there was a moments silence for reflection from both parties.

"Why do you want to go back to work Alex?"

"Because of what we know Mr Mellor? You have just told me there are eleven times the cases out there that I first thought." There was a plea in Alex's voice.

"That's not the real reason is it Alex?" Mr Mellor was almost smiling at her now.

"Of course it is, we have a job to do. You said it yourself your colleagues on the board are happier knowing we have someone out there trying to clean this mess up. Let it be me. You know I can do it. I have at least proved that too you?"

"They do and we do, I know you can do it Alex, your one of our own." Alex let those words stay in her head a while, she didn't really know how to take that comment.

"One of our own?"

"Yes Alex!" Alex looked at him smiling back at her and then at Oliver, Oliver shrugged his shoulders and gave Alex the look as if to say he had no idea what he was on about.

"I am not a Brown Institute baby Mr Mellor? Is that what you mean? I would know, believe me I checked."

He was still smiling, Alex didn't like it. This was making her angry again.

"They are not all babies Alex. As I said before, it's been twenty years. Do you not think we have got better, and more efficient in what we have achieved? About three months ago when you came to me with this cock and bull story about getting it wrong, and my son Michael was a good lad just at the wrong place at the wrong time. Did you not think I knew what he was? Didn't think that I knew where he was from? You wanted to go to Germany, you wanted to go to my institute. There was a fire in your belly Alex I could see it. I could see that you were like a dog with a bone it's in your nature. We had been discussing for a long time how to start to clear some of this up. And you were my perfect opportunity, my own little trial." Alex stood up, Oliver pulled his gun in front of him and so did Christopher.

"Sit down Alex, you said you wanted to know everything and I am telling you everything. You aren't a Brown Institute baby… you're a Brown Institute adult Alex. When you arrived in Germany at the institute. You had your little tour and lunch with Jonathan Smith. Then what?"

Alex was thinking back. They went back down stairs and separated for the tests.

"We had the tests?"

"No, your friend, Chris Masters he was tested. What we did Alex was more than that to you. You had a pre sedative in your food at lunch and in the saline drip we put you on before we tested you there were more sedatives. That knocked you out for about an hour. We performed an operation on you and implanted synthetic DNA directly into you." Alex sat silent trying to contemplate what Christopher was saying.

"Alex you don't need to work. That's not what you are craving, you need to kill." Everything fell into place. The need for the work. The sickness in the stomach when she wasn't on a case. All of it had start to become clear. She was one of them. She was what she was hunting.

"Bastard." Alex was up and jumping towards him. Christopher pushed back the chair and held the gun directly at Alex's head. Oliver's gun was also pointed out in front of him.

"Sit down, Alex. Sit Down!" Alex backed up. But didn't sit down.

"How is that even fucking possible?"

"Alex it's possible because we make it possible, we are months away from developing the technology to change DNA with a single injection." The synthetics were working over drive in Alex. All she could think about was grabbing that gun and killing both of them there and then.

"Can you imagine Alex, killers not mine but the real ones. Ones who already have the genes. What if we could make them better, if we could actually kill their instincts with kindness?"

"You made a cure? You said it wasn't possible." Alex's only thought now was how do I get cured. She had forgotten the fact that there was a good chance that she was dead within the next hour.

"It wasn't back then. Now we are making an antidote. It won't cure you but it will enhance your other feelings which hopefully by the very nature of feelings will squash the desire. Imagine what people would pay for that?"

It was money and power again. Christopher was out of control. He could now make a killer and cure a killer. Alex knew she needed to deal with him. She wanted to kill him. She was a killer. She hadn't been on a quest, she had been on a killing spree. Alex kept running through her head all the killers she knew. Female killers, there wasn't many. Was she it? Was she the most notorious female killer of them all? What had they done to her?

"This is all about money? And power? Why did you do this to me, I have neither?"

"Because I knew you weren't going to let it lie Alex. Forgiveness isn't in your nature. I needed to ensure I had something to control you with. It's what has brought us to this moment Alex. I know it can be controlled as long as there is a purpose. You gave what we did a purpose and it was acceptable to you. That means it will be to others also. I am sure you are better knowing the truth before you pass on? Aren't you?" Alex wasn't ready to pass on. There were more institutes, there was Christopher and the board to deal with along with the thousands of others.

"I am still an asset."

"You are an asset that the president of the United States knows about Alex I can get another." Alex knew that was right. He wasn't going to let her live, not now. If it was as simple as to make and injection to create a killer, he didn't need her anymore.

"I think it's time," Christopher stood up. So did Alex they were almost face to face again.

"If you are going to do it then I want to see the look in your eyes as you do. I want to know that we both die killers Mr Mellor. Although only one of us is going to hell."

Christopher had the gun pointed at Alex's chest.

"I am not a killer Alex." Alex was perplexed as he was standing in front of her with a gun in her ribs.

"Oliver," Alex could see Oliver walking towards them over Mr Mellor's shoulder.

"No, you do it, you pull the trigger, come on be a man." Alex's blood had started to boil now she could feel the rage through her body, she wanted to tear his head off but she knew between the two guns in the house and a half a dozen outside this was it. The end had come for her.

"Be a man Christopher, be a man!" Alex was almost shouting at that point. Christopher took a step back as Oliver approached Alex. Oliver raised one hand to his earpiece and with the other lifted his gun and placed it against Christopher Mellor's head.

"Step forward again sir."

"What, Oliver, what are you doing"

"Forward now," Christopher did as he was told.

"What are you doing Oliver?" Oliver didn't reply to him.

Alex didn't say a word. Oliver then reached into Mr Mellor's Jacket and pulled out the silver plate gave it to Alex.

"Hold it on your shoulder it will show the same height to the people outside to the door." Alex did what she was told.

"Oliver you have to be kidding me, you know we cannot let her go. We have to follow through on this or else it will be us that gets it next. You heard what the board said. This is our job to clear this mess up. You know that. We can't let her live."

"You can't, I can" Oliver pulled the trigger and one of the cogs in the Brown Institute stopped turning.

Chapter Sixteen

"I know I should be thanking you, but what was that about?"

"He deserved it Alex, it's been coming a long time and I tried to tell you all this but you didn't listen to me. Keep that plate on your shoulder." Oliver reached over and pulled it up a bit on her shoulder

"They will think there is just the two of us still standing. They can't get a good outline due to the old style house with the big bricks but they can get a reading off of these."

Alex flung her arms around Oliver.

"I thought I was done," he pushed her straight back.

"We maybe yet. There are five of them out there. And don't hug me, well not yet it's not a thing that me and Mr Mellor do very often."

"Good point, I have something to ask you? Do you think he was telling the truth about the synthetics?"

"I am afraid he was Alex. He explained it all to me on the ride over here. He told me he thought his little experiment had gone wrong. Now I know what he meant. I knew about the injections and how far they had come. I just didn't know they had done it to you."

"Bastard, and the institutes?"

"That's true too Alex, I was going to tell you everything I knew after the Curle farm and, well the night that followed. It's why I left the laptop out to show you. I didn't expect you to wake up I was only gone a minute. But I can explain all that later first of all we need to deal with these people outside."

Alex just nodded. Oliver was in charge. After the last hour's events Alex didn't have a straight thought in her head.

"Help me put Christopher's body on the chair, that way it will look like he is sitting down. Leave the plate on his body and walk backwards in a straight line to the sofa and play dead. I will open the curtains and beckon them in. There are five of them. They will leave two outside covering the door. I will be behind the door and will take the two outside you will need to take the three in here. There weapons won't be drawn so you will have the element of surprise on your side. Don't miss and take them down." Oliver remembered who he was speaking too, not only was this something she did on a daily basis but she had just found out it was in her DNA.

"Okay." They set about the plan. It worked as the three guys walked in Oliver was outside and had the two guys in his sight. He waited until he heard the gunfire from inside before taking them down. He didn't want the men inside spooked and drawing weapons on Alex. As soon as they were down he returned to the house. Alex was stood in the centre of the room. The three guys were all down and dealt with.

"We are good?"

"We are." Oliver walked over and kissed Alex. She was a mess, the emotions of the last hour were hard to take and here she was with the man she had been missing, kissing in the middle of an eight time murder scene.

"We need to go, there needs to be some distance between us and the White House and all of this as soon as possible."

"Okay but what do we do about all this?"

"We torch the lot of it. Let's get all the bodies in a room and set fire to it. Hopefully it will take them a long time to work out who is who. That will give us some time to make our escape."

"Okay."

Alex did as she was told and laid all the bodies out on the floor one by one. Oliver dragged the two from outside. Alex went to the kitchen to find something to start the fire with, there was alcohol but that was about it. Oliver turned up with a petrol can from one of the SUVs outside. They covered the bodies and the curtains in petrol and set light to the living room. When they arrived at Alex's car, Oliver just got into the driver's seat. Alex got into the front next to him. They headed west they needed to get out of state and fast. A few minutes into the journey Alex looked over at Oliver with tears in her eyes.

"Thanks."

"For what exactly?"

"For saving my life, again. I really thought that was it tonight."

Oliver just smiled at Alex. He leant over and pushed his hand over her cheeks to wipe away the tears.

"Anytime, let's get some distance and decide what we do next?"

"I am really not sure, but I could do with a drink."

Alex laid back on the seat as Oliver drove and was asleep within twenty minutes. Oliver drove as far as he could until his eyes were struggling to see the road. He stopped and checked them into a motel. They slept till noon the following day. When they woke in the morning they were in bed fully dressed and holding each other on the bed.

It was less than twenty minutes before they were no longer dressed.

If they would have switched on the TV instead they would have heard the breaking news.

"At precisely one a.m. this morning Police and fire crews were called to one of the homes belonging to Secretary of State Robert Henderson. There were reports of an actual fire and gun fire at the home. It is believed that they have recovered at least eight bodies, one of which is said to be his son, another local billionaire Christopher Mellor, five of his security detail and the body of an unknown woman. Police at this time are treating this as suspicious circumstances."

Two days later Victoria Owens was sitting in the oval office working on papers for a new treaty in Ghana. There was a knock on the door.

"Come in."

One of her security guards entered and handed her a phone.

"It is her Madam President." The president held the phone to her ear.

"Hello, okay. Come here to the White House. Tell them your name at the security point they will bring you directly to me."

The president handed the phone back to the guard.

"She will be here in thirty minutes ensure with Karen that my schedule is clear. Doesn't matter what else was in there."

"Yes, Madam President."

The guard nodded and walked out of the oval office. The president sat back in the chair.

Thirty minutes for Victoria Owens felt like a long time. She had been expecting the call sooner. They had identified the mystery woman but they hadn't released that detail to the press. She knew Alex was still alive. She just hoped she was going to come forward and help her with her problems.

Almost on the thirtieth minute the door to the oval office opened and the security guard entered.

"She is clean, Madam President"

"Thank you Lee, you can leave us." He left the room and closed the door behind him.

"You may be clean young lady, but I do have one question, who are you?"

"My Name is Dee Quaid Madam President." Dee took out a hard drive from her purse and placed it on the table.

"I think you are after what is on this drive. Alex Keaton came to see me a few weeks ago after visiting her parents. She told me she had even more proof about the Brown Institute, she told me about Mr Mellor and she told me about the files and the killings and Michael and Jonathan Smith. She told me about the true avengers and the secretary of state's son. She told me if anything was to happen then I was going to come and see you. She told me this and nothing happened, and then she came back." Dee had gotten herself in a state. Everything was happening so fast and now here she was sitting in front of the president of the United States.

"I think I have some of that, are you okay dear do you need a glass of water?"

"No I am fine," Dee tried to compose herself,

"Just upset, and she came back, and she said, she said, she had worked it all out. And it was to do with money and power and the Stapleton's and then she said she had to do something, but she gave me a phone and said this was a direct line to you. And then I saw the news, only last night I was on a painting trip down by the lake. I would have come sooner but I didn't know I didn't know that he had got her." Dee was getting more and more upset. Her speech was almost babbling now.

"Who had got who Mrs Quaid?"

"Mr Mellor and the fire and Alex being dead."

"She is not dead Mrs Quaid, that wasn't her in the house. It was a young lady from the neighbourhood."

This stopped Dee in her tracks. She had got herself worked up about this over the last twelve hours and couldn't think of anything else.

She had blamed herself for her death. It had all started with her husband. He was the reason that she was involved in this. He was the reason. But now Alex was alive. Dee started to cry.

"Are you sure?"

"Yes we are sure, I thought it was her who was coming here today. You sounded very similar on the phone."

"Sorry I should have told you. She said to use her name if I needed you. So that's the one I used with the guard." Dee was calming herself down now.

"It's all fine now Mrs Quaid, can I call you Dee?" Dee nodded at her. Victoria Owens had a way of putting people at ease.

"Let me order us some tea and a sandwich and you can sit here and tell me all about it. Start to finish. I have cleared my schedule. But just not as fast as the last five minutes please." Victoria Owens smiled at Dee. She picked up the phone and ordered some refreshments. They arrived and they moved from the oval desk to the sofas in the centre of the room.

"Okay why don't you start Dee?"

Dee took a sip of her tea and placed it down.

"It starts with my late husband," Dee paused at the word late. It had been nearly four months since Jack's suicide and a year since they were really together. Those memories started to flood back to Dee.

"His name was Jack."